MAX AND THE
SNOODLECOCK

Book Two of Max and the Multiverse

A novel by Zachry Wheeler

ISBN: 978-0-9982049-4-9
Edited by Jennifer Amon
Published by Mayhematic Press

For Evelyn, who suffered
through every dumb name
before snoodlecock.

CHAPTER 1

Given that space wants to kill you dead any chance it gets, space stations stick out as peculiar feats of ingenuity. In simple terms, they are little more than fragile atmo-boxes floating inside a vacuum. They rely on complex systems to stay afloat, where if the tiniest thing goes wrong, death lurks outside like a hungry badger. This is why they embody the *function over form* methodology, where a potent desire to remain living trumps everything else. Still, one would think that somewhere along the line, space station management would take a long hard look at their homely air tank and think *hmm, maybe some drapes.*

Despite this hideous baseline, the Durangoni Station of Leo stood out as one of the prettiest ports in the entire Virgo Supercluster. From a distance, it resembled a polished top, the kind children play with for about eight seconds before succumbing to boredom. Its silvery exterior shimmered in the blackness of space like a warped disco ball. Due to its massive girth and gravitation, the station could not orbit a planet. It had to *be* a planet. Thus, it floated around an orange dwarf star as an artificial sixth in a family of five, lingering on the outskirts like a neighbor child that always showed up for dinner.

As visitors neared the station, many battled an outbreak of zarbopplement (a word unique to the station, denoting a potent mixture of shock, awe, vertigo, and a sudden desire to contemplate the meaning of life). Thin fissures encircled the structure, splitting it into countless horizontal sections. They expanded little by little before revealing themselves as entry points to colossal rings of commerce. The central rings housed an infinite variety of common markets. Venturing to the outer rings required discerning tastes, peculiar interests, or straight up fetishes. The smaller the ring, the smaller the audience. For many creatures, the tiny rings of Durangoni offered a safe haven in which to indulge in life's stranger things. Known as the Kink Rinks, they provided an endless bounty of freaky fodder.

A constant flow of planetary traffic poured in and out of the central rings. Each level sat a full kilometer away from the next, allowing the passage of every sized vessel, even massive battlecruisers. Every ring attached to the inner core, a fixed pillar that stretched from pole to pole. Inside, a dedicated community of engineers maintained all structural and life support systems. Their talents kept the enormous edifice afloat, so they enjoyed a rock star status wherever they went. Many spent their entire lives aboard the station, content to live out their worry-free careers.

The sheer scale of Durangoni gave it both gravity and atmosphere, allowing most visitors to walk along its surfaces unprotected. An elaborate reclamation system provided an optimal mix of breathable gases. The surfaces of center rings housed artificial lakes, sandy beaches, mountains for winter sports, and a vast array of amusement parks. Their modular frameworks allowed designers to swap and shuffle, drawing a regular influx of cash-laden tourists.

A transparent security barrier enclosed the station in upper orbit, serving as a checkpoint for all planetary traffic. An army of port controllers managed the ceaseless transit. Ships descended in stacked lines through entry gates and redirected once inside, like a deck of cards dealt from the bottom. From there, visiting vessels punched through the atmosphere like any other planet and floated down into the various ring divisions.

The shadow of a central ring swallowed a tiny freighter as it kicked towards a pre-approved landing pad. The boxy ship sailed by the control tower of a lumbering cruiser and zigzagged through a small fleet of maintenance craft. The edge of a landing pad glowed green as the ship neared the ring wall, a titanic pane of viewports, service hatches, and docked vessels. Thrusters ignited, spilling blue flames from the hull and slowing the freighter to a gentle hover. Three clawed legs gripped the smooth metal service, completing an easy arrival. The white glow of twin rear boosters faded into nothing as the main engines spun down for an extended stay.

Inside, two orange Mulgawats, an Earth human, and a cyborg cat prepared for a routine restocking mission. Ross, a curled ball of chubby marmalade, rested upon a guest cabin bed. The landing thump lifted him into the arched stretch of every cat ever. He leapt down from the bed and trotted into the cargo bay. The charcoal walls and metal floor echoed his stride, highlighting the emptiness of dwindling supplies. In the rear of the bay, Max sat upon a cargo crate while staring at the wall. His maroon shirt and scruffy brown hair stood out as lonely pops of color inside a stark gray canvas. Ross pranced over to his longtime companion and gazed up to find a puzzled expression.

"Oi, what's wrong?" Ross said.

"I can hear colors," Max said, his bulging eyes darting between the gray wall, a piece of purple fruit in his hand, and his navy blue pants.

"Yes, your synesthesia. What about it?"

"My synes—huh?"

"Your synesthesia?" Ross glanced away and shook his head. "You know, the condition you've had your entire life? The one where you hear colors? What's the problem?"

"This is an *actual* condition? I thought I had acquired some D-list superpower."

Ross started to reply, but his brain declined and volleyed back to the mouth. "*What?*"

"The purple fruit sounds like psychedelic funk, the gray wall sounds like German techno, and my blue pants sound like, well, the blues. I hear Muddy Waters every time I look at my crotch."

Ross lifted an eyebrow. "Your strange is strong today, my friend."

"Everything I look at has a background theme, which, it seems, is all based on color." He glanced down at Ross and snorted. "You sound like elevator music."

Ross rolled his eyes. "Ugh, not even going to bother with this today. You're on your own, Nutty McNuisance."

"Ooo! Green!" Max leapt to his feet and pointed a finger around the cargo bay. "Let's find something green. I bet it's Kermit singing *It's Not Easy Being Green.*" Max unlatched a large crate and dove inside.

Zoey emerged from the cockpit and paused at the sight of Max's legs dangling from atop an open crate. She hooked a thumb on the waistband of her cargo pants and squinted through a sunburst complexion. The matte blue scales along her neck reflected the overhead light as she tilted her head. They disappeared under a sturdy leather jacket that hung from her shoulders. She took a deep breath and exhaled a heavy sigh, stretching a thin blue tank top across her chest.

"What the hell is he doing?" Zoey said.

"Looking for colors," Ross said with a flat tone.

"Pink sounds like pop diva garbage," Max said, his voice muffled inside the crate. "No surprise there."

Zoey raked a hand through her choppy black hair and glared at Ross.

"Don't look at me, I'm not his therapist."

Max popped up from the crate holding a bright green canister. His giddy grin withered to a frown. "Aw, sounds like reggae. Which, I guess makes sense." Max tossed the canister back into the crate and met eyes with an irritated Zoey. "You also sound like elevator music."

"Who sounds like what?" Perra said, peeking around the engine room door. A long auburn ponytail swung across her shoulder. She wiped her face with a tattered rag, exposing a toothy smile and creamy orange skin.

Max glanced around the group. "You all sound like ads for anti-depressants."

Perra cocked her jaw and eyed Zoey, who shrugged and shook her head. The buckles of her machinist pants clanked against the doorframe as she stepped into the cargo bay. She slid a wrench into her pocket and wiped her hands on a grease-stained halter top.

"Is he going to be okay outside?" Zoey said to Ross.

"Why are you asking me?"

"He's your human, isn't he?"

"What, like I keep a leash in my pocket?"

Zoey huffed. "Just keep an eye on him, would you? We have a lot to do today and little time to do it. I would rather not babysit a neurotic human."

"Guys," Max said with a cocky undertone reserved for stock-brokers. "I'll be fine, don't worry."

"Don't forget," Perra said to Max. "You and I have some hard-core shopping ahead of us. We have a mess of parts to find. Still have that list I gave you?"

"Yup, right here." Max fished a piece of paper from his pocket and stared at it like a drunk with a breakfast menu.

"You okay?" Perra said.

"White sounds like country music." Max scrunched his brow, then grinned. "Oh, I get it. That's pretty funny. Good one, brain."

"Okay then," Zoey said, quelling the room with a firm clap. "We all have shit to do, so let's get a move on. I want us locked down and ready to depart in 10 marks."

"Can do," Perra said.

"Aye aye," Ross said.

"Yanni," Max said.

The group responded with puzzled stares.

"*That's* what you all sound like. *Yanni.*"

* * *

Seven shadowy figures in crimson cloaks sat in silence around a large table, its round surface glowing with a faint diffusion of light. They traded glances under sagging hoods, their expressions shrouded in mystery. One member sighed with impatience. Another twiddled her thumbs. The head member, occupying a pointy throne, stared straight ahead with ashy hands resting on the table. Wall sconces flickered behind the group, casting slivers of light along the tarnished metal. The chamber radiated with a solitary purpose, one that spurned decorations or a simple refreshments table.

The crackling static of an incoming transmission broke the dead air. The cloaked ensemble stirred in their seats as the hologram image of a reptilian humanoid pieced itself together above the table. Battered pauldrons rested atop a suit of thick leather, giving the beast a warring demeanor. Red eyes scowled beneath a frayed headband, channeling every villain from every kung fu movie. It held an elaborate polearm by its side, for whatever reason one might need a spear in space. The scaly creature bowed, cleared its throat, and offered a report.

"Master Fio," it said with the classy tone of a debutante. "We have a confirmed sighting at Durangoni Station. The ship has docked for resupply, however brief."

"Who do we have in proximity?" Fio said in a squeaky high-pitched voice that caused everyone to wince.

The lizard paused for thought. "Hmm, the Qarakish of Leo would be the closest."

Fio grunted and stroked his chin. "No, they would never make it in time. I shall summon the Orbed Enforcer."

Gasps and murmurs lifted from the table.

"Silence!" Fio slammed the table with a pudgy fist, his shrill voice assaulting ears like a valley girl at the beach. "I have made my decision."

The whispers ceased.

Fio flattened his hand and returned his attention to the reptilian beast. "Thank you, Becky. Stand down and await further instruction."

"Yes, Master." The lizard bowed before crumbling into a wash of static.

Fio erupted with a devious laugh, mirroring the shrieks of a terrified rabbit cornered by a hungry puma.

* * *

Max and company tromped down a service gangway towards a vast bazaar, one of the countless market hubs inside Durangoni Station. The interior glistened under a sheen of nonstop care. The occasional maintenance droid weaved in and out of pedestrian traffic, groaning and chirping like an overworked housemaid. Mumbles of conversation filled the tunnel with a dull roar. An intricate filtration system pushed clean, cool air through the complex. Diffused panels along the ceiling blanketed the corridor in sterile light.

Max grinned as he studied the endless variety of alien visitors hiking alongside the group, each with their unique background music. He started to enjoy his mental jukebox, seeking out the most colorful combinations he could find. A striped serpent with reds, yellows, and greens caught his attention.

"Yo, check it," he said to Ross. "That snake dude sounds like bagpipes."

"That's not a dude," Ross said.

"That's a—how can you tell?"

The creature tossed a stink eye to Max.

"They also have exceptional hearing," Ross said.

Max offered a timid wave of apology. "I thought snakes were deaf."

"That's racist," Ross said, cocking an ear back.

Max huffed and stopped in his tracks, halting the group and angering every alien behind them. The sudden obstacle drew grouses and curses from passing patrons. Max shook his head and glared at Ross. "What is it with you and this obsession with political correctness? Furthermore, how can a statement of *fact* be racist? Snakes are deaf. How is that offensive?"

"Because I'm not a *snake*," the serpent said, now standing (in a manner of speaking) behind Max, its tiny T-rex-style arms folded in the universal form of disapproval.

Ross sat in silence while Max fumbled through some life experience.

Max grimaced, then turned to the creature. "Um, well, you *do* look like a snake."

"Oh, so we all look alike to you?" The serpent inched closer, bringing them face-to-face.

Max froze, heeding his brain's demand to *STFU*.

Zoey applied a vigorous facepalm.

Perra inserted herself between Max and the creature and offered a consoling smile. "I am so sorry, please excuse our ignorant companion. He has only been off his planet for a few pochs. He doesn't know any better, but we're trying our best to teach him. Thank you for this growth opportunity and I hope you can forgive us."

"He's an asshole," the serpent said.

"No arguments here," Ross said.

Max, still paralyzed by ineptitude, shot a glare at Ross.

Zoey rubbed her forehead, trying to massage away the sting of embarrassment.

"We will do our best to educate him on the intricacies of interstellar relations," Perra said. "I promise."

The creature sighed. "Very well, a good day to you."

"And to you."

The serpent nodded and slithered away.

Zoey punched Max in the shoulder hard enough to leave a temporary bruise of shame.

Max recoiled. "Ow! What the hell?"

"What have we learned?" Ross said, using the mocking tone of a grade school teacher.

Max sighed and shook his head. "Let's just go."

The group soldiered down the corridor, melding back into the flow of traffic. The drums of a vibrant marketplace filled the tunnel as they neared the exit. Max jerked his head from side to side, peering over scaly shoulders for a sneak peek. His curious mind recalled the unrestrained chaos of Hollow Hold, its filthy markets echoing the shrieks of shady merchants. Durangoni Station embodied the polar opposite side of commerce, one with sleek designs, clean concepts, and unspoken rules of civility. It reminded him of the mega malls back home, minus the screams of feral children.

Near the exit, a lengthy section of tunnel flickered from light to dark, much like the beginning of too many horror movies. A maintenance humanoid with yellow skin, baggy overalls, and a trucker cap fiddled with a bundle of wires sticking out of a wall panel. His tentacle mustache shifted back and forth as he tested the voltage. Caution cones and a cart full of tools created a bottleneck of foot traffic, pushing everyone to the opposite wall. Visitors shuffled through the faulty segment without a second thought.

Max tucked his shoulders as he and the group entered the glitchy section. He glanced up to the defective lighting strip. It blinked off, hurling him into the wall with a harsh thump. With each flash, Max yelped and slammed himself into the wall. Zoey grabbed him by the collar, yanked him through to the other side, and tossed him to the floor. His back hit with a hard thud, drawing a final yelp.

"What the hell is wrong with you?" she said.

"Black is death metal," Max said, rubbing his neck.

Zoey narrowed her eyes.

"You know, angry music. Headbanging, mosh pits, an uncontrollable urge to punch your neighbor."

She balled her fist and shook it at Max. "You're about to get punched right here."

"Calm down," Perra said, extending the proverbial olive branch. "No harm done, he's just a little wonky today."

Zoey yanked Max to his feet and threw him into Perra's arms. "Fine, you babysit him then."

Perra sneered at Zoey. "Well aren't you grumpy today," she said, then tossed Max back to the floor.

Ross sighed and started grooming his paw.

"This isn't a pleasure trip," Zoey said. "We have a lot to do and he's turning into a liability, *again*. We should have left him on the ship."

"To do what? Pick his nose? Break something? I need the extra hands and it's not like he's useful by himself."

"I'm right here guys," Max said from the floor.

"He's *your* problem," Zoey said. "*You* deal with it."

"Fine, I will," Perra said through a sour gaze.

Zoey turned for the exit and stomped away.

"Don't mind her," Perra said to Max. "She gets like that when time is a factor. She doesn't do well with derailment."

"Noted," Max said, then climbed to his feet.

They resumed their walk, leaving a reasonable distance between them and Zoey.

"So what is that thing you said ... a *mosh* pit?"

"Oh, um, think of it as a swirling fight club set to heavy music."

"Sounds dangerous."

"Depends on the music."

The group exited the tunnel into a massive marketplace brimming with activity. A sea of sentient creatures flowed in every direction. The entire social spectrum churned inside a cauldron of retail. Elegant gowns and dapper suits floated towards posh restaurants. Leather jackets with sling packs and thick utility belts scanned the peripherals for bargains. Strange beasts with curious eyes browsed the colorful wares like tourists at a flea market.

The giant round room housed shops and boutiques of every style imaginable. Prominent establishments lined the rear walls with large hologram logos hovering above the entrances. A crowded assortment of kiosks filled the center, selling everything from snacks to novelty items. Bombastic merchants in loud attire pestered passersby with the same overhyped sales pitches understandable in any language. They twirled gadgets, pushed samples, and boasted about the latest greatest whatever.

A web of walkways, tube trams, and elevators connected all the markets. From a general perspective, most customers could locate everything they needed within a small radius. Patrons often chose their docking point based on the rarest item in their list, then acquired everything else from adjacent markets. On occasion, they needed to travel between rings to complete their purchases. If necessary, the station provided a complimentary shuttle service, but for the most part, they docked once and stayed put. Should a curious patron pick a direction and start walking, the shops would start to repeat themselves after a mile or two. Durangoni Station existed as a planet of perpetual trade where if something didn't exist there, it didn't exist at all.

Max wandered through the market in a marveled daze, like a dog trying to grasp object permanence. Widened eyes followed an array of chandeliers hovering along an open ceiling, emitting ethereal tones similar to Gregorian chants. His dangling jaw and rubberneck stare gave him away as a newcomer, not that it mattered. Durangoni Station was a safe harbor, a neutral sanctuary that offered goods, services, and nothing more. In order to safeguard their wealth and reputation, the controlling faction employed a private army that rivaled most militaries in the quadrant. With a stern hand and a watchful eye, they dealt with everything from orbital assaults to shoplifters. In addition, their expansive monitoring system put most galactic casinos to shame.

"C'mon," Perra said, grabbing Max by the forearm.

They rejoined Zoey as she paused to consult her comdev.

"Do you know where you're going?" Perra said.

"Yeah, I think so." Zoey scanned the area and pointed to a nearby archway. "That passage leads to Courier Corner where the PCDS outpost is located. Maybe we can pick up an extra item or two. After that, I'll swing by a medi-shop and meet you guys at the nutri-mart below us."

"Sounds good. I should be able to find all the parts we need without venturing too far. There's a big machining warehouse two floors above us. They have a nice selection of converters at decent prices, so I'll stock us up. Max is going to look for em-panels and flark switches."

Max nodded, having no idea what she meant.

"Good," Zoey said. "Oh and if you see a—"

"Zoey Bryx!" said a guttural voice from across the way.

The group turned in unison. A crowd of dainty tourists parted to reveal a large hairy beast with meaty paws resting on its waist. Bloodshot eyes with red irises stared through a pair of bushy black eyebrows, resembling giant caterpillars caught in a fur trap. A set of stumpy horns poked through a brown mane that disappeared beneath a gaudy leisure suit. Flashy jewelry and a silky undershirt completed the portrait of a mobster yeti. The creature nodded and smirked like it owned a devastating secret.

Ross cocked an ear. "Who in Tim's Blue Hell is that?"

Without a word, Zoey steeled her gaze, balled her fists, and stepped towards the beast.

CHAPTER 2

A tiny stealth ship floated outside of Durangoni Station, its dark hull lost in the blackness of space. The round vessel resembled an overgrown eight ball, minus the eight. A narrow slit served as a viewport and glowed with a deep shade of red. A Mohawk of tarnished antennae gave it the unsettling persona of a punk rocker gone to the dark side. Under a veil of silence, the ship pushed towards the station without a spray of thrust or kick of fire.

The ship sailed by orbital traffic and slipped through a barrier gate like an underage teen ducking door bouncers. Beacon scanners remained silent. The vessel wasn't there as far as Durangoni was concerned. The station housed one of the most sophisticated security systems known in the 'verse, and yet, the tiny stealth ship made its bold approach without a care in the world. It dipped and weaved around shuttles and carriers, pushing towards the surface with the stony confidence of a drunken redneck.

Even gravity seemed aloof to the stealth ship's presence. It glided through the atmosphere without the glow of entry flame. The pilot opted for a night-side approach, as anyone with functioning eyeballs would wonder why a giant black ball fell from the sky. Once inside the atmosphere, the ship continued to puzzle physics, emitting no sound whatsoever. Hurling itself towards the ground, any reasonable onlooker would assume the engines had failed, dooming the vessel to a deadly thump. However, the ship slowed to a comfortable hover above its target, the slotted doors of a small service tunnel atop one of the central rings.

The viewport pulsed, commanding the tunnel doors to unlock and slide open. The ship floated inside and the doors closed behind it. The black ball zipped around bends and corners while skirting security sensors with its advanced cloaking technology. It sailed through junctions with the composure of a Pac-Man pro. Lighting strips snapped over the hull like passing floors in a speedy elevator. The vessel dipped, ducked, and dived before arriving at its destination, a maintenance shaft above a central marketplace.

It exited the tunnel with a gentle drift and floated down to a maintenance pad, slowing to a stop above the surface. The ship locked itself into a magnetic hover without the use of landing gear, just a big black ball defying gravity with a giant middle finger.

A nearby worker halted a patch weld, turned for its tool cart, and flinched at the sudden appearance of a menacing round ship. The startled creature removed its helmet and plunked it on the cart, rattling the tools on top. A confused gaze probed the dark vessel. Slitted eyes peered through a scaled complexion while a forked tongue tasted the air for trouble. Worry gave way to curiosity, drawing the worker over to the hovering ball. It studied the unresponsive ship for a moment before succumbing to irritation. The creature sighed, adjusted its sweat-stained crew shirt, then slammed a fist into the hull.

"You can't park here! Maintenance crew only!"

A sliver of crimson light split the ship in two, expelling a sinister hiss. The worker backtracked a few steps as the top half detached from the base and lifted into the air. Another black orb rested inside, like a Russian nesting doll. A pair of glowing yellow eyes materialized. They blinked and studied their surroundings like a newborn chick before whipping a death stare to the maintenance worker.

The reptilian yelped and scampered away.

* * *

The hairy beast stiffened its posture as Zoey closed in. He lowered his hulking arms, balled his fists, and gritted his teeth with anticipation. Zoey maintained her laser-like focus, her stride heavy with purpose. With a few steps left between them, she lunged forward and buried her fist deep into the beast's stomach, folding him forward and dropping him to a knee.

"Barfin' napkin parka!" the creature said, vomiting every ounce of air inside his lungs. He wasn't referring to actual barfing napkins or parkas. It's just what his cursing sounded like in whatever language his brain blurted out.

Zoey snort-laughed as the beast coughed and wheezed.

"Where the—*cough*—bleeding hell—*hack*—did you learn that?"

He raised a paw while continuing his intimate study of the floor. Zoey snatched the fuzzy mitt and yanked the beast to its feet. She wrapped her arms around him and giggled like a schoolgirl.

"It's so good to see you, Gamon."

"You too, girl—*cough*—I'll have to toughen up for next time."

"That's nothing. You should see Perra throw a punch."

"Who am I punching?" Perra said as she strolled up.

Gamon let out a hoarse chuckle, exposing nubby teeth inside his plump jowls. He grabbed Perra by the shoulders and yanked her into a rocking embrace. She giggled through a drapery of arm fur, squeezing the beast with all her might. Max moseyed up with hands in pockets and a curious gaze. Gamon's eyes widened. He released Perra and snatched the human by the face, devouring his head with a hairy palm. Max barked and flailed as the beast conducted a thorough examination.

"Where did you find an Earthling pet?" Gamon said to Perra. He cupped the back of Max's head, plunged a finger into his mouth, and swirled it around like an empty pint of ice cream.

Max gagged and pummeled the beast's arm.

"Picked him up on Europa," Zoey said in a flat tone.

"He's in great condition too," Gamon said while testing Max's elbow strength.

"Little help, ple—" Max said before Gamon jabbed his stomach with a meaty finger. Max crumpled to the ground, coughing and wheezing.

Gamon grimaced. "Kind of weak, though. No matter, their flesh is delicious."

Max yelped and sought refuge behind Perra's legs.

Ross perked with interest.

"And who's the other one?" Gamon said, pointing at the cyborg feline.

"That's Ross," Perra said. "He's Max's pet."

Gamon donned a puzzled expression. "The pet ... has a pet?"

"Not a pet," Max said in a strained voice.

"Also not a pet," Ross said.

"Technically," Zoey said, glancing away with a twinge of embarrassment, "they're crew."

Gamon nodded with a half-grin and a scrunched brow, as if his face muscles refused to agree upon the conveyed emotion.

"I'm showing him the greaser ropes," Perra said. "He and Ross got entangled with us back on Europa. Long story, ended up at Hollow Hold and—"

"You came from *the Hold*?" Gamon perked with notable interest. "Big news on the wires, you hear about Halim? He was hiding out there, had a big battle with the Varokins before some wily assassin took him out."

Zoey raised her hand. "That was me."

"That was you what?" Gamon said.

"That was *me*. I shot Halim in the face with my plasma pistol."

"You shot—" Gamon morphed between vexation and concern, twisting his fuzzy face into an array of troubled expressions. He scanned the immediate area for prying eyes, then leaned into the group and lowered to a whisper. "We need to talk."

Gamon gathered the group and led them to a nearby pub. The beast took point, carving his way through the thick crowd with little effort. Most stepped aside at first glance of the approaching wall of fur. Those that didn't received a stiff shoulder and the disapproving glare of an orange house cat. Rounding a final corner, Gamon paused to survey the area for any suspicious attention.

Plain white pillars and steel railings outlined the exterior of the pub. A hand-painted sign with bright alien lettering extended a warm welcome. The group stepped through the entrance one by one and followed Gamon through a near-empty room of rustic tables and chairs. The place emitted a weathered yet cozy vibe, the kind of pub beloved by locals but dismissed by tourists. Dark wood panels encased a slab bar along the side wall, housing a fat amphibious bartender who wiped a glass underneath a haughty expression. He nodded at Gamon as the group passed, conveying the visual equivalent of a secret handshake.

The group settled into a large mafia-style booth at the rear of the establishment. The table overlooked an open-air garden that spanned five levels of the complex. The vibrant vista bustled with fountains and pedestrians. Exotic trees sprouted from angular potting rows. Thick leafy vines with colorful flowers hung from a suspended trellis far above. The open balconies of numerous restaurants surrounded the garden with the pub resting on the third floor. A dull roar of conversation lifted from the churning crowd, shrouding the booth in privacy.

Zoey scanned the garden, then turned a sharpened gaze to Gamon. "Okay, so what's wrong?"

"Just to be clear," he said, lowering his palms to the table surface. "You killed Halim."

Zoey met eyes with a worried Perra, then returned her gaze to Gamon. "Yes."

The beast rapped his fingers and took a needed breath. "Then you're in danger. Someone has not taken kindly to the death of Halim. Word is, an assassin has been deployed to assassinate his assassin."

Zoey's eyes widened. "I'm a mark?"

"Looks to be."

"Who's the banker? Nifan?"

"No. Halim was a pawn. Essien was the prize. Nifan disappeared shortly after the battle. No one has heard from her since."

"That doesn't make any sense. Who the hell would even care? I killed the greatest war criminal that ever lived. I did a service to the universe. Even the Council of Loken gave me a crisp thumbs-up."

"No arguments here. Grats, by the way."

"Thanks."

They bumped fists.

"Doesn't matter though. You're marked and the hit is in play. But, you should be safe for now because no one seems to know who the assassin is."

"Who, my assassin?"

"No, *the* assassin."

"Me assassin?"

"Yes, you assassin, not your assassin."

"So not the other assass—"

"Stop saying *assassin*," Max said with a curt tone.

"Ass," Ross said. "... assin."

Perra snort-chuckled.

The front door exploded off its hinges and slammed onto the floor, kicking up a cloud of dust. A handful of customers screamed and darted for the nearest exits. The bartender grunted, tossed his rag onto the counter, and strolled into the kitchen with the urgency of a snack break. A scraggly humanoid at a side table gripped his mug and leaned back in his chair, undeterred by the invasion yet intrigued by the ensuing shenanigans. The group spun their heads in unison and gawked at a giant black blob with glowing yellow eyes filling the doorway. Ross poofed his fur, about-faced, and leapt over the booth railing. A tiny fountain splash echoed from below.

The blob squeezed itself into the pub, its bloated mass wobbling atop a pair of stumpy legs. The floor groaned with every heaving step, like an elephant atop an old hardwood floor. A quick scan uncovered the group in the rear booth. The creature narrowed its gaze and lifted a plasma pistol with its noodly arm. Instinct drove Zoey's hands under the table and flipped it onto the floor, facing the metal surface towards the blob. The intruder opened fire. Plasma blasts careened off the table as the group cowered behind for cover. Purple streaks zipped overhead, carving through hanging vines and dropping them to the garden floor. The crowd erupted in chaos, fleeing for their lives as plasma fire ripped through the canopy. Screams and explosions echoed around the complex.

"Fire back for fuck's sake!" Max said.

"Neutral station, idiot!" Zoey said. "No guns allowed!"

"That's a dumb rule!"

"You're a dumb rule!"

"That doesn't make any sense!"

"Can we not do this now?!" Perra said.

Gamon peeked around the table, only to dodge another barrage of plasma fire. The blob lumbered forward, shaking the floor with each step. Gamon wrapped his palm around the table pedestal and pointed at the railing.

"Follow the fuzzball. I'll cover you."

Zoey gripped his shoulder and nodded a grim *thank you* before hooking Max with both hands and heaving him over the railing. A high-pitched scream ended with a belly flop into the fountain below. Perra followed him down and Zoey leapt behind her, each slipping into the water with the grace of Olympic divers.

With a strained grunt, Gamon hoisted the metal table to his waist. Plasma blasts slammed into the surface as he leaned into the weight and gave charge, tromping towards the black blob standing near the entrance. Sweat poured from his furry brow. Lips tightened around his teeth. A mighty yawp escaped his chest as he barreled into the orb with all his strength. The table bounced off the bulbous creature and clanked upon the floor, tossing Gamon off to the side in an awkward tumble. The fleshy mass, unmoved in every sense of the word, eyed Gamon with an ominous gaze and chuckled like a nightmarish boogieman. It lifted a noodly appendage and pointed at the felled beast, only to discover that the impact had disarmed it. The blob grumbled and scanned the floor for its weapon. Gamon scampered to his feet and escaped out the front door.

Ross shook himself dry while Max clawed his body from the fountain like a swamp creature. Zoey and Perra emerged beside him and vaulted over the rim, flinging arcs of water onto the floor. The crowd had dispersed in the panic, leaving them to the echoes of a cavernous room. Max scanned the level, uncovering winding paths, twisting trees, and banks of curious foliage. Zoey hooked his arm and yanked him to his feet.

"Keep moving," she said, then sprinted towards a tunnel overhang.

The group followed close behind, stamping wet prints on the polished concrete. They rounded a corner and paused to regroup behind an abandoned snack kiosk.

"What the hell was that?" Max said while trying to catch his breath.

"The door greeter," Zoey said, then smacked the back of his head. "Did you really just ask that question?"

"Oh, pardon me for wondering why a jelly monster was shooting at us."

"Shut up." Zoey hugged the wall and peeked around the corner back towards the garden.

Perra peeked over her shoulder.

Max peeked over hers.

Ross peeked around Max's calf.

A colorful chicken-like creature peeked around Ross.

"Bacock!" it said.

The entire group flinched in unison.

Ross re-poofed and skittered against the wall.

The bird stood its ground while jerking its gaze between startled faces. A cluster of blue snoods jiggled beneath an orange beak. Its feathers spanned the rainbow, everything from shimmering reds to iridescent purples. A thick crest of white fuzzy strands gave the bird an Einstein-like persona. "Bacock!" it said again, this time more agreeable.

The group traded puzzled glances.

"Why is a disco chicken yelling at us?" Max said.

"Beats me," Perra said.

"It sounds like RuPaul."

"Who's RuPaul?" Zoey said.

"A talented dude lady back on Earth with big hair and flashy outfits," Ross said.

"That sounds fun," Perra said.

The black assassin rounded a far corner, riding a hover scooter about three sizes too small. The poor contraption struggled to keep its occupant afloat, accenting each floor scrape with a shrill error ping. The creature lifted a plasma pistol and squeezed the trigger. The group dove behind the kiosk as purple streaks zipped down the tunnel. Max caught a glimpse of the approaching brute, which sounded like a fusion of speed metal and ukulele.

"We're trapped," Perra said.

Zoey scanned the area between blasts. "Shit."

The kiosk shook with every impact, raining alien snacks upon the group. Out of nowhere, the creature howled and slammed the scooter into the wall. Zoey peered around the booth to find the bird flapping atop the monster's head, pecking furiously at a pudgy face. The blob bellowed while flailing its noodly arms, trying desperately to rid itself of the pest. The plasma pistol fell from its grasp and clanked upon the floor.

"Bacock!" the bird said, then chomped down on a finger.

The beast shrieked and shook its hand in stinging pain. The bird flapped as it soared through the air, attached by beak to the blob's flesh. A rainbow of feathers floated to the ground around the wrecked scooter.

"Let's go," Zoey said. She leapt to her feet and sprinted down a connecting hallway.

Perra nabbed Max by the hand and yanked him into a gallop. Ross followed close behind. The group tore through tunnels on their way back to the ship. They sailed around a final corner and into the glitchy gangway. Max cringed as he passed into the blinking section. The sudden pops of death metal drew yelps and stumbles. He staggered through the section, cursed its mother, and resumed a full sprint.

The group arrived back at the ship gasping and panting. Perra opened the airlock with a remote command, allowing everyone to leap into the cargo bay without breaking stride. Zoey retrieved a plasma pistol from a nearby locker and returned to guard the airlock. Perra darted into the cockpit to begin launch prep. Ross settled into a quiet corner and started grooming his ruffled fur. Max stood in the center of the cargo bay with hands on his knees, trying to catch his breath. Zoey braced herself behind the airlock with pistol locked onto the landing bay entrance. For once, Durangoni lay silent, and the eerie calm elevated a sense of dread.

"Launch prep complete," Perra said.

"Gravy," Zoey said. "Let's get the hell out of here."

She holstered her weapon, hurried into the cockpit, and threw herself into the pilot seat. Speedy hands buckled in, seized the yoke, and slapped the thrusters icon. Blue flames spilled from the hull, lifting the ship from the platform and tilting it skyward. Zoey slid a palm up the console, igniting the main engines. The sudden blast warped the landing pad and kicked the freighter towards the sunlight above. Soon after, the flashes of Durangoni patrol ships appeared in the distance. They grew brighter and brighter, then zipped by without interest. Zoey and Perra traded relieved glances as they exited the station rings and sailed into the atmosphere. The viewport faded to black as the vessel slipped through a barrier gate and into open space.

"We're clear," Perra said.

"Initiating jump sequence," Zoey said while tapping the console.

Max climbed into the cockpit and strapped himself into a wall seat behind Zoey. Ross leapt into his lap as the jump indicator pinged green.

"Everyone hold onto something," Zoey said and slapped the icon.

"Roger that," Max said.

"Good to go," Ross said.

"Bacock!" the bird said as the ship disappeared into a sliver of purple light.

* * *

The black blob sat on the floor of Durangoni Station, its puddled mass leaning against the wall next to a smashed scooter. A skinny arm reached above its glowing eyes and grasped a zipper atop its head. With a steady tug, the beast unzipped the glossy suit, exposing pale skin, sunken eyes, and rows of chubby chins. He pulled the zipper down to a sweaty chest, then flopped his arm onto a rotund belly. Exhausted beyond words, the brute gasped for air like a beached whale. A splotchy bald head lifted through a thin mane of sandy brown hair, like a traveling salesman way past his prime. Red bumps peppered his face, the painful remnants of his feathered assailant. He wiped his brow and fished inside a pocket for his comdev. A few taps created a hologram image of a conference table surrounded by robed figures.

"Silence!" Fio said in a squeaky voice from the head of the table. "The Orbed Enforcer beckons the Council! Speak, brave warrior."

"Still not fond of that name," the beast said in a meek voice.

Fio huffed. "Oh c'mon, Jerry. We agreed that you needed a cool nickname."

"I never agreed to that."

"But we voted on it," said another robed tablemate.

"No, *you* voted on it. You also made me wear this stupid getup. It's way too tight and it makes me sweat something fierce."

"We also gave you a nifty weapon," another figure said.

"Doesn't change the fact that I can't feel my crotch."

"Enough!" Fio said. "Report your status."

Jerry groused and rolled his eyes. "Found the group, had a battle, they escaped."

"The Earthling escaped?!" Fio's voice elevated to mouse squeal.

"What did you expect?! I'm a particle physicist, not an assassin!"

The clomps of Durangoni troops echoed down the hall, hooking Jerry's attention. They rounded a nearby corner and crouched into assault formation, aiming their plasma rifles at the gelatinous blob leaning against the wall. Their black suits and polished helmets stood out in sharp contrast to the warm market surroundings.

"Obese intruder," an officer said. "Put your tentacles on your head and turn ... well, um, just put your tentacles on your head."

Jerry ignored them. "Did you hear that? Durangoni just called me fat."

"But you *are* fat," Fio said.

"Well yeah, but, why bring that up in a standoff? It's unprofessional. I shoot this place all to hell and Detective Douchnozzle calls me a fatty."

"Durangoni does not discriminate," the officer said with a hasty delivery that screamed *oh shit I'm so fired.* "We are a proud and diverse unit that arrests equally."

Jerry sighed, then gestured to Fio. "Anytime, dude."

"Oh, right. Fiona!"

"Yes, oh wisest one, knower of all things, sexiest sexpot in the known universe," said a breathy feminine AI voice.

"Initiate transfer of Jerry."

"At once, Master."

Ribbons of blue light swirled around Jerry's beefy body. Moments later, a glowing cocoon yanked him into the ether, leaving a pool of sweat beside a broken scooter.

CHAPTER 3

The tiny freighter floated in the blackness of space under the veil of a silent beacon. Its twin rear engines glowed with an idle hue, blending into a backdrop of stars. Inside the cargo bay, the group stood together in silence. Zoey gnawed at her cheek with arms crossed. Perra shifted her lips under a taut brow with hands tucked inside her pockets. Max scratched his head, perplexed as always. Ross wore a stoic expression, conveying mild concern or total disinterest. (Nobody could ever tell, to be honest.) The flamboyant bird in front of them, however, jerked its gaze around the group as if curious yet apathetic.

"Why is a snoodlecock chilling in our cargo bay?" Perra said.

"Wait, you know what that thing is?" Max said.

"Of course. They're quite delicious. I can only assume he escaped from one of the restaurants back on Durangoni."

The snoodlecock bobbed its head, then pooped.

"Ugh," Zoey said, crumpling her face.

"I'm not cleaning that up," Ross said.

Max snorted. "As if you would."

Ross shot him a stink eye. "Are you saying I'm lazy?"

Max responded with a *duh* arm spread. "Dude, you are the laziest thing I have ever known, human, feline, fictional, or otherwise. And that's coming from a goddamn *gamer*."

Ross pursed his jowls. "*Yeah*? Well, you're a—a wanking wanker."

"Nice comeback, Garfield."

"That's racist."

Perra sighed. "Are you guys done?"

Max and Ross traded scornful glares, then returned their attention to the matter at hand. The snoodlecock indulged in a brief flapping fit, freeing some feathers.

"Bacock!" it said, startling the group.

"That is going to get really old, really fast," Perra said.

"So let's just eat him," Zoey said.

"*Eat* him?" Max said with a horrified tone. "But the little guy saved our lives."

"So? It's still a tasty treat."

Perra raised her hand. "I know a good recipe."

"Might I suggest," the snoodlecock said in a baritone voice well-suited for documentary films, "that we reassess the nature of our relationship."

They all turned stunned gazes to the creature.

"Bacock!" it said, then pooped again.

* * *

A restive silence gripped the dim conference room. The door slid open, revealing a massive creature shrouded in a crimson cloak. The Orbed Enforcer loomed as a frightening fiend, at least for a moment. Six shadowy faces turned to greet him, or rather, went to an absolute minimum effort to acknowledge his presence. He pushed his bulk through the frame, resulting in a few squeaks of exertion. The cold stares of the group followed his mass around the table to an empty seat. Floor panels whined under each laborious step. Wall sconces rattled, as if to fat-shame him with jolts of flickering light. Jerry dropped his rotund body into an oversized seat. The impact jostled the table, resulting in irritated mumbles. His crimson hood slipped off his head, unveiling a splotchy scalp and impressive chin collection.

"Ahem," his robed neighbor said.

"Huh?" Jerry turned his giant skull.

The neighbor tugged on his own hood.

"Oh, sorry." He flipped the hood back into its menacing position, then stiffened his posture and clasped his hands in a desperate attempt to regain said menace.

Six cloaked faces maintained their disapproving stares. One shook its head and another sighed before their gazes slogged back to the center.

Fio cleared his throat and raised his hand, quelling the room. "Let us begin. Please raise your hands to the ordained position of regard."

"Can we just skip this crap?" a hissing voice said.

"Agreed," another said. "The commencement is dull and meaningless."

Fio stuttered, then slammed a fist onto the table. "How dare you balk at Suth'ra tradition!"

Jerry sighed. "The Suth'ra have no tradition. That's, you know, kind of the point."

"Jerry's right," another said. "The society was founded under the guiding principle that there *are no principles*. We do, act, and study as we please. This opening ceremony crap is a direct violation of Suth'ra principle."

"But if there are no principles," Fio said with a snarky tone, "then how can we violate a principle?"

An awkward silence responded.

"Aha!" Fio slapped the table surface. "Victory is mine! The ceremony shall beg—"

"Let's put it to a vote," Jerry said, removing his hood in defiance.

"Agreed," his amphibious neighbor said, removing her hood as well.

The rest of the group, minus Fio, removed their hoods, exposing a bundle of bizarre faces. Eye stalks traded glances without moving their respective heads. Forked tongues and striped tentacles crawled over rough scales and nappy fur. Despite the compilation of tones and body types, the group still managed to radiate complete nerdom.

"No vote!" Fio said, leaving his hood untouched.

"Why not?" Yerba said with one mouth, then switched to the other. "This isn't a dictatorship."

"It ain't a democracy either," Fio said.

"If I had to define it," Carl said, musing like an arrogant historian, "I would call it a totalitarian version of anarchistic soc—"

"Shut up, Carl!" Fio said. "Everyone knows that we are a lawless assembly of—"

"To be fair," Gorp said with a throaty grunt, "Carl has a valid point. While many of us would define the Suth'ra as an autocratic regime of sorts, there is an essence of chaotic rule that chooses to govern itself."

"Yes, indeed," Frank said, nodding his eight-eyed head. "The organization does have a tyrannical vibe similar to a constitutional monarchy, but minus the unnecessary strains of a parliamentary republic. In my humble opinion, it acts as an untethered oligarchy."

The group turned puzzled gazes to Frank.

Kaeli raised her one hairy eyebrow. "That was, like, a Wikipedia entry entitled *All the Governments.*"

Frank sulked. "I just wanted to participate."

Jerry raised his hand. "All in favor of deprecating the Ceremony of Pleasantries say *aye.*"

"Aye," said everyone but Fio.

"Then it's settled," Jerry said, thumping the table. "We shall no longer say *hello* to start the meeting."

* * *

Max and Perra sat atop a pair of cargo crates, their faces drooping with disbelief. Ross leaned back against one of the crates while grooming an outstretched leg. Zoey stood off to the side with her eyes pinched closed, rubbing her forehead as if dealing with the sudden outburst of a bigoted uncle. The snoodlecock pecked at a piece of lint stuck between the cargo bay floor panels, its bright orange feet and dark talons gripping the metal grates. An occasional flap unsettled the group and dispersed colorful feathers around the room.

"So let me get this straight," Zoey said. "You swapped bodies with a snoodlecock in order to escape a mob faction who wants you dead for boinking the boss's daughter."

"Yup," the bird said without breaking its rigorous study of floor filth.

"And your previous body, a reptilian thug or whatever, is about to get whacked back on Durangoni Station."

"Yup."

"And you don't want it back?"

"Nope."

"Why not?" Perra said.

"Escaping was a top priority. I'll take another body when I need to."

Zoey hardened her gaze. Perra lifted to her feet and took a wary step back. Max tumbled off the crate and scrambled up to a karate stance. Ross cocked his ears back and gave the bird a long, hard stare. The snoodlecock shot its head up and traded glances with the apprehensive crew.

"Oh, yes, I forget that's a frightful statement. My sincere apologies." The bird cleared its throat. "I am a Yarnwal of Yankar. We are a semi-clairvoyant race with the ability to inhabit the consciousness of other life forms. However, the target needs to be of lesser cognizance or an unused shell of my original species. To put it another way, unless you have some dim-witted pets, you need not worry."

Ross glanced over to Zoey. "Does Max qualify?"

Max huffed. "Shut up, ass."

"No, I'm serious," Ross said, retaining a soft sincerity.

Zoey smirked while Perra chuckled.

The snoodlecock stiffened its posture as if to channel a drill sergeant. "My name is Gerfon Temparstangle Folinster Er Domplefoosh, but you can call me Steve."

Perra fished her comdev from her pocket and dove into research.

"Okay ... Steve," Zoey said. "I'm Zoey and this is Perra, Max, and Ross."

"Huh?" Ross said, lifting his head from his crotch.

"Nothing," Zoey said with an eye roll. "Go back to not caring about anything happening."

"Roger that," Ross said and returned to his crotch.

"He checks out," Perra said while scanning the output of her comdev. "Either he is who he says he is or he's a damn good liar. But, given the nature of our predicament, I don't see any reason not to take him at his word."

Steve bobbed his head.

"Still," Zoey said. "I would like to get a second opinion. In the meantime, we need to figure out what to do with him. Call me crazy, but I'm not comfortable with a mind melder running around the ship."

Steve flapped a fresh round of feathers into the air. "If it will make you feel better, I am happy to remain quarantined inside a guest cabin."

"Seems reasonable," Perra said.

"But we only have two cabins," Max said.

"Your point?" Zoey said, tossing him an unsympathetic glare.

"Well, I can only assume that you two aren't sleeping in the cockpit, so what am I supposed to do?"

Zoey narrowed her gaze. "I dunno, figure it out?"

Max huffed, pouted like a scolded child, then turned for the guest cabin he shared with Ross. He grumbled under his breath as he slipped through the door. Steve watched with minor interest before returning his full attention to Zoey.

"Yankar is my home planet," he said. "It is located on the outskirts of the Perseus-Pisces Supercluster. You can plot a course f—"

"No," Zoey said. "We're on our way to Ursa Major *and* we're marked by unknown assassins. With all due respect, I don't know you and I don't trust you. You'll get off at our next port and go where you please."

Steve moaned. "Awe c'mon. Don't make me say it."

Zoey clenched her lips.

"Say what?" Perra said.

Steve glanced away and shook his head. "She's going to make me say it," he said to some cargo netting as if it could burst into life and take his side.

Zoey glared at him, then gestured to get on with it.

Steve huffed. "Fine. I saved your life. You owe me."

"Ha!" Max emerged from the guest cabin with a wad of linens underarm and a mattress dragging behind. "Sweet, delectable karma." He dropped a sour gaze to Steve. "Enjoy the cold floor, bed stealer."

Steve glanced at the mattress. "It would seem to me that *you* are the bed stealer."

Max stammered, then dropped the mattress. "You know what I mean, dammit!"

Ross smirked. "Not to point out the obvious, but if the bird is clairvoyant, what difference does it make to lock him inside a cabin? You could toss him in a spacesuit and float him in the black, wouldn't make a damn bit of difference."

Zoey glanced at Perra, who shrugged and nodded.

"Just give him the cargo bay and lock up everything else. And besides, if he's going to shit all over the place, I'd rather it be in here."

"Good point," Zoey said.

"Works for me," Perra said.

"You slow-rolling bastard," Max said, then grabbed the mattress from the floor and dragged it back into the guest cabin.

* * *

Fio grumbled at the head of the table with all eyes locked on his cloaked visage, anticipating a response. He shifted in obvious discomfort, trying his best to wrangle some menace. Stony eyes reflected the soft glow of the table surface. Wall sconces flickered with the ambience of a dungeon, filling the room with malaise. Fio rapped his fingers upon the table, as if pondering a poker move. The galloping taps of fingernails amplified the tension. His chest raised and lowered beneath a statuesque stillness. After a long stint of contemplation, he balled his hand into a fist and slammed it upon the table.

"Fine!" he said. "From this moment onward, we will no longer use *literally* when we mean *figuratively*. Anyone caught using the terms incorrectly will be banned from the High Council meeting for three sessions."

Mumbles of satisfaction floated around the table.

Fio expelled an over-exaggerated sigh. "I am *figuratively* melting with rage that you grousing ninnies have *literally* pissed away hours on this nonsense. Can we get on with the meeting now?"

"Well, you can't *literally* piss time aw—"

"Shut up, Carl!" Fio jumped to his feet and flipped his hood, exposing ashy skin, nubby horns, and a pudgy round face. He pointed a rigid finger at the yellow humanoid. "So help me, if you say another goddamn word, just *one*, I will *literally* clip those eyestalks and feed them to Jerry!"

Jerry perked up.

Carl puckered his fishy lips.

Fio's gaze darted around the table. "Anything else?"

Silence responded.

"Good." Fio plopped back into his throne. "Now, on to the matter at hand. The Earthling remains unfettered. The Orbed Enforcer has failed us."

"Oh fuck off, Fio," Jerry said.

Fio whipped a wide-eyed death stare to Jerry. "Excuse me?"

"You heard me, bro. I *literally* just told you to fuck off." Jerry added a visual aid, a crook-fingered gesture known to his species, but foreign to everyone else at the table. "You stuffed me into gimp suit and sent me to acquire an Earth human from a pair of highly trained PCDS couriers. What the hell did you think would happen?"

"You ungrateful turd! We gave you a highly advanced stealth ship and a highly advanced weapon to combat those highly trained couriers."

"You can also mount a laser to a wiener dog, don't make it a good idea."

An awkward silence ensnared the room. Jerry and Fio traded heaving scowls, piercing each other with resentment. Everyone else froze. Suth'ra members, as passive-aggressive weirdos, regarded petty disputes with the same paralyzing fear as stumbling across a bear in the woods. Every so often, tensions built to a fever point, requiring a skilled diffusion to retain peace. Luckily, Jerry held a black belt in nerd fu.

"Do you want a donut?" he said.

"I would love one," Fio said.

The group exhaled a collective sigh and rose to raid the snack cart.

* * *

A small bank of asteroids floated in empty space, content to twist and tumble without a care in the world. Every now and then, a wayward rock would bump another, creating a brief bout of pinball chaos that ejected an innocent boulder. More often times than not, the rock floated away into the black abyss, never to be seen again. Some wander into solar systems and become permanent additions to orbital debris. Some disappear into black holes. Others slam into habitable planets and exterminate giant reptiles.

A tiny freighter ship floated alongside the asteroid field, spinning with a slow pitch as a pseudo rock. Inside, the dim cockpit glowed with the yellow hues of scanners. The vessel remained in stealth mode with the control panel showing an array of disabled systems. The occasional ping of a passing ship echoed around the cabin, oblivious to their presence. Zoey and Perra slipped through the narrow passage and into the cockpit without a word, their mirrored faces taut with concern. They dropped into their respective seats and started prepping the ship for departure.

"So what do you think?" Perra said as she strapped herself in.

Zoey took a deep breath. "Well, he's locked in the cargo bay, which is the best we can do at the moment. I dunno, feels like my stomach is tied in knots. I'd much rather be focusing on the whole *assassin* thing." She closed her eyes and plunked her head back onto the headrest. "A smooth-talking snoodlecock is an unfortunate distraction. But he's right. He saved our lives and we have to honor that. We have a debt to repay."

Perra spun up the engines and jump drive, maintaining focus on the console. "We gonna take him home?"

"Maybe." Zoey tightened her buckle straps. "I think we should run this by Phil."

Perra groaned and grimaced.

"Trust me, I know. But given the situation, what choice do we have?"

"Fair enough." Perra lowered her gaze and shifted to a somber tone. "Any word on Gamon?"

Zoey frowned and shook her head. "No. I pinged him through every latent proxy I could find, but nothing yet. Of course, that could mean anything. Maybe he's lying low. Maybe Durangoni is on lockdown. Who knows? I can't do any real recon without blowing our cover."

"He made it out," Perra said with a hesitant nod.

"I truly hope so."

The jump icon pinged green, breaking the sullen silence. Zoey gripped the yoke and thrust the ship away from the asteroid field. She tapped coordinates into the console and thumped the icon with a limp fist. Perra grasped her hand as a sliver of purple light engulfed the ship.

CHAPTER 4

Evolution is the improv comedian of the natural world. It just rolls out mutations and hopes for the best, like a blind man playing darts. Its shtick may receive praise, ridicule, or slack-jawed confusion. Some ideas are great. Take eyes for instance. Seeing is pretty darn cool. Some are not so great and end up in the slush piles of biologic history. And yet, some mutations slip through committee and leave everyone dumbfounded. Notorious examples include Galwock's 42-fingered goobergobble and Earth's duckbill platypus.

And then there was Phil, evolution's booby prize.

Phil was *literally* the only sentient being on his planet, and remained that way for billions of years. His original species, a simple form of unicellular pond algae, enjoyed life on a relatively inert planet. It had beautiful landscapes, a balmy climate, plenty of freshwater, and a healthy amount of sunlight. But, the world was chemically barren, not that the algae minded. It's not like they yearned to be anything other than algae. The planet simply enjoyed them as algae and the algae enjoyed the planet enjoying them. Thus, the partnership persisted.

That is, until Phil evolved a random neuron.

Burdened with a shiny new thinky part, Phil decided that floating in a sunlit pool wasn't interesting enough. He started to pulsate, which pushed his single-celled body in different directions. This amused Phil, so he decided to keep the mutation. Yes, *keep*. This particular algae species enjoyed a peculiar form of immortality. Every few months, the cells regenerated from the inside out, rebirthing themselves over and over and over. They could even revert to a previous iteration, like ditching a crappy new operating system, not that any of them did. The difference between one version and the next was, well, nothing. But in Phil's case, it gave him a unique superpower. If he fancied a new mutation, he could keep it forever. If not, he could discard it and go back to a previous version, like balking at the latest smartphone in favor of your tried and true.

And therein lay Phil's monumental hardship. While all his asexual siblings floated in ponds thinking about nothing of concern, Phil was busy trying to figure out a good use for tails. Year after year, century after century, era after era, Phil mutated and rebirthed himself. Running was fun, until he tired of it. Flying was a blast, until he tired of it. Telekinesis was a fabulous party trick, but he had nobody to show it off to.

Before long, depression set in. Thinking persisted as the only activity he enjoyed. As a result, he shed many of his mutations in favor of general maintenance. Or rather, he let them atrophy like a dodo bird giving the middle finger to flight. After all, he had seen every nook and cranny of his planet a million times over. He was bored. And depressed. He took the form of a gelatinous blob, basically a giant brain encased in flesh and apathy. He did keep the ability to roll, because an annoying itch is no fun for anyone.

Phil thought and rolled around his lonely planet for millions of years. Then, on one fortuitous day, he acquired the ability to absorb radio signals. A curiosity at first, he enjoyed the tickle of static until he uncovered some notable patterns. He forged numbers into mathematics, then shapes, pictures, words, and language. The entire universe opened up to him, turning apathy into elation. An endless stream of data flooded his ravenous mind. He learned about stars, planets, galaxies, aliens, the whole enchilada. Giddy beyond words,

Phil decided to belch his own radio signals into the cosmos, hoping to converse with his newfound neighbors. After all, he had all the time in the world to await a reply.

Everything was peachy awesome, at least for a time. Phil spent his days tidying up the planet on the off chance that someone might fancy a visit. He arranged rocks, cleaned out caves, and sought the best landing plots. He obsessed over tiny details, smoothing dirt and scooching pebbles into more aesthetic positions. The hulking mass wandered the planet in search of things to spruce, like an eager grandparent on the cusp of winter break. During the evenings, he stared up into the sky, wondering if and when the time would come.

And then, after eons of rolling, cleaning, and dreaming, Phil received a response.

Being alone for billions of years and then suddenly not is a thrilling proposition. That is, until you discover just how unbelievably stupid everyone else is by comparison. Phil, a brain blob with a billion-year study history, pulsated at the opportunity to chat with another sentient being. But, his enthusiasm faded after receiving his first batch of replies. No advanced mathematics or quantum theory, just an "oh hai" followed by reality shows, news feeds, and romcoms. Phil spent years dissecting the signals, desperate for any signs of intelligence. He was appalled by his thinking brethren, like Einstein trying to make sense of a Kardashian.

Phil came to the sobering conclusion that he was the smartest being in the known universe, and indeed he was. The stupidest among his connected civilizations deified him, much to his chagrin. He would have rolled his eyes, but he had de-evolved them a million years prior. Most regarded him as a curiosity, like a caged animal across the cosmos. Instead of engaging his intellect, they just wanted to know how he pooped. The smartest civilizations sought to milk his wisdom, like a jock cheating off a nerd's exam.

Depression returned. He stopped sending out signals in favor of a monk-like isolation. The occasional Suth'ra signal tickled his interest, but not enough to kick the funk. Most of them fell onto deaf ears (or rather, an internal collection of fleshy radio antennae). He thought and rolled, rolled and thought, content to live out his days in solitary confinement. A hundred years passed. Then a thousand. Then a million, and another million. Time marched on, indifferent to the ceaseless sorrow it wrought. But then, halfway through the fifth million, something extraordinary happened.

One day, a spaceship broke through the tranquil clouds and floated down to the surface. Nothing hostile or brazen, just a simple shuttle with common components. The crew, a small group of transporters passing through the system, had no interest in harming or exploiting the planet. They just needed to refresh their water stores. The ship settled next to a large lake, lifting shimmering waves in the bright sunlight. A pair of amphibious humanoids exited the ship as the main engines spun down. They unlatched a hose, dragged it over to the beach, and plopped it into the water. An automated filtration system siphoned the water it needed. A simple pit stop, then back to the black.

Phil watched them from afar, like a curious kid with a magnifying glass. (In lieu of eyes, Phil's skin absorbed the entire color spectrum from gamma to radio. It could also change color, shape, and adopt alluring textures. Not that he knew what constituted alluring, although his favorite form resembled a flamboyant koosh ball.) Disguised as a boulder, he marveled at the presence of other thinking beings, despite their inferior intellects. As the crew completed their task and prepped for launch, Phil found himself overwrought with an emotion he didn't fully understand, a fierce longing of sorts. At that moment, he broke his silence.

"Please don't go," Phil said through telepathy.

The pilot, a greenish humanoid with bulging eyes and a comically large mouth, turned to her co-pilot and scrunched her brow. "Huh?"

"I didn't say anything," the co-pilot said.

The pilot turned and eyed the small crew sitting behind her. "Who said that?"

Shrugs and confused looks responded.

"That was me," Phil said to everyone, his tone sheepish yet pleasant.

The startled crew shot worried gazes around the cabin.

"Who the hell is that?" the pilot said with a mixture of shock and annoyance. "Yanthu, if you're doing that damn ventriloquist thing again, I am not amused. Impressed, yes, but not amused."

"Not me, boss," Yanthu said, adding a brow lift.

"Again, it was me," Phil said.

The entire crew, minus the co-pilot, flinched in unison. The co-pilot was too busy prepping the ship to get the hell off the creepy planet. His spidery green fingers blurred atop the console. An array of status icons reflected off widened eyeballs that screamed *shit-shit-shit*.

The pilot took a slow breath. "And who, might I ask, is *me*?"

"You are Renny," Phil said.

Renny narrowed her eyes. "No, I mean, who are *you*?"

"Oh, yes. My name is Phil. I live on this planet, which I have named Phil's Place. And might I add with the utmost hysteria, it is an acute pleasure to meet you all."

"Meet us? We don't even see you. Are you in the ship?"

"No."

"Then where are you?"

"On Phil's Place."

The pilot sighed. "No, I mean, where are you in regards to our ship?"

"Oh, my apologies. I am disguised as a giant flesh rock on the hill behind you. And if I might be so bold, it would be an explosive thrill to touch each and every one of you in the most intimate of fashions."

All eyes grew wide with horror.

Renny joined the co-pilot in *shit-shit-shit* launch prep.

An enthusiastic Phil shed his craggy exterior for a more natural fleshy state, then spun into a frantic roll down the hill. *Goody goody goody* he thought as his bulky mass carved through the dirt and flopped over rocky terrain. The shuttle, having reached launch capability in record time, ignited its thrusters and hovered above the ground, kicking up a cloud of dust. Renny punched the boosters icon, spewing pillars of flame from the rear. Phil, having none of it, blasted the ship with an electromagnetic pulse that fried all of its circuits. The engines died and thrusters ceased, thumping the lifeless hull back onto the ground. Moments later, Phil's beefy mass skidded to a halt just outside of the airlock.

"Are you ready to meet your new best friend?" Phil said with the giddiness of a newly adopted puppy.

The crew screamed as Phil ripped the airlock door off the ship and hurled it into the lake behind him. After a distant splash, everyone quieted to find a pink blob pulsing outside the door. Horrified faces morphed into twisting expressions of confusion, disgust, and total bewilderment. Phil quivered with uncontrollable excitement, like a bowl of gelatin on a rickety rollercoaster. Tentacles shot out of his body, one for each crew member, and stopped in front of their chests. The ends formed hands and assumed the customary handshake position.

"Intimate touching! Intimate touching!" Phil said. (He recalled television signals where friends greeted each other with cordial handshakes. Having never learned what the gesture was called, he took his best guess.)

The only crew member not paralyzed with fear reached out and gripped a hand.

Phil exploded in what could only be described as an atomic orgasm, billions of years of isolation coming to a shattering climax. A violent release of energy rumbled the ground and refried every circuit in the ship. A surge of pops and sparks filled the cabin. The crew covered their heads as tiny embers bounced around the interior. The vessel smoked and dimmed, leaving a parched shell in the dirt. Phil, now a quivering wad of post-pleasure, expelled a fluttering sigh and melted into a fatty pool at the base of the ship. A crude bubbling sound accompanied the dissolution. If he could have lit a cigarette, he would have.

An enticing new world had opened itself to Phil. Even the smartest beings in the universe needed to connect in some meaningful way. As a rolling brain pillow with infinite capacity, Phil had never considered such a need until it presented itself by chance encounter. At that moment, he understood the power of raw desire. At least, to an extent. Young men understand that there is a biological drive to touch anything that looks soft and seductive. But, a set of unspoken social rules keep hands in pockets. Phil, as the sole inhabitant of his own planet, never benefited from knowing these rules. Ergo, he became every social creature's worst nightmare, an awkward creep with a complete disregard for personal space.

This posed several problems for would-be visitors. Once word got out about Phil and his planet, beings from all over the universe wanted to meet the all-powerful knower of all things. Unfortunately, Phil garnered a reputation for being a bit "handsy." In perhaps the most ironic of twists, Phil had no sexual desires of any kind. All he wanted were hugs, handshakes, and the occasional back rub. But, his teen-like persistence and clumsy approach unnerved every visitor that set foot on the planet. Before long, his visits slowed to a trickle. Most beings viewed extended stays as too high of a mental price.

Phil slipped back into a mild depression, having no clue why everyone avoided him. He rolled around his planet, mumbling snarky comments like a preteen with popularity troubles. Regardless, he always perked up whenever ships dropped by. Those who continued to visit needed confident personas, fresh towels, and a high tolerance for weirdness. Phil's favorite guests included Morgok the World Crusher, Toby (an intergalactic chess prodigy with rage issues), and a pair of no-nonsense couriers named Zoey and Perra.

* * *

Max awoke as a sentient toothbrush with a pink bowtie. Four wiry limbs ended with white gloves and black booties, much like a vintage cartoon. A fierce desire to weave baskets infected his mind, which made little sense until he glanced around the stark white room. Straw baskets of every shape and size lifted to the ceiling. Even his straw bed featured an intricate weaving pattern, something he paused to admire with loving strokes. A bristly plastic head sat atop a slender body that bent like soft taffy. He lifted to a sitting position, or whatever position constituted sitting for a large flexible toothbrush. Luckily for Max, this particular waking involved little more than a full bladder. He would be fast asleep in a few short minutes, so he wasted no time. He climbed to his polished feet and paused in the middle of the room. Having no idea how or where a toothbrush urinated, he proceeded to relieve himself where he stood. A warm stream crawled down his leg, but no liquid was visible. A curious sight, but not enough to warrant any further examination. His sleepy brain chalked it up to *don't want to know* and left it for his brushy alter ego to deal with. He yawned, returned to bed, and drifted back into nothingness.

* * *

Max awoke a few hours later in his familiar guest cabin. A quick glance around the room confirmed the gray panels and simple doorframe. The silky sheets fell to his stomach as he lifted onto his elbows. A wad of orange fur stirred at the foot of the bed. Max grinned and swung his feet to the cold metal floor. An eye rub and lip smack greeted the new day.

"Morning, alright," Ross said, then lifted into an arched stretch.

"Morning," Max said.

"Fikarek, alright," Ross said, prompting the far wall to render transparent.

The tendrils of a fiery nebula crawled across an ocean of stars. The pale dots of a distant asteroid field twinkled like sun-drenched sand.

Max studied the visage with a cheeky grin. "Never gets old. Goddamn the universe is a beautiful place."

"A beautiful place that will ghost you without a second thought, alright alright."

Max groaned with the realization that a new question needed answering. He slumped forward, clasped his hands, and debated on whether or not he wanted to know. But his curiosity, always a goading temptress, quelled any chance of blissful ignorance. He sighed and turned to Ross. "Why do you keep saying *alright* like a sly Texan?"

Ross lifted an eyebrow. "I was going to ask the opposite, alright. Why did you stop, alright?"

"You sound like Matthew McConaughey."

"You mean *President* McConaughey, alright. Show some respect, alright alright."

Max huff-chuckled and rubbed his forehead. "You have got to be kidding me."

"I do not joke about the single greatest US President to have ever graced the office, alright. The guy is a legendary hero, alright alright."

Max leaned upon his elbows and dropped his face into his hands. "I know I'm going to regret this, but ... why is, President McConaughey, a hero?"

"What, do I look like a historian, alright? You studied his regime in school, alright alright."

"His reg—*really*?" Max tossed a WTF gaze at Ross, then shook it off. "Just humor me, alright?"

Ross smirked. "Alright alright alright."

Max rolled his eyes.

"From the McConaupedia," Ross said, then cleared his throat and switched to a 50's era documentary tone. "US President Matthew McConaughey presided over the greatest era of peace and prosperity ever achieved on planet Earth. He united all nations under a global treaty of progress and cooperation. His numerous triumphs include curing cancer, eliminating poverty, and increasing overall life expectancy by 30 years. McConaughey was the only President to serve five consecutive terms, made possible by an overwhelming universal demand. While elected to serve a sixth term, he stepped down in order to lead the first manned mission to Mars, where he became the first human being to set foot on the red planet. Before his death in 5-603-114, he led a global initiative to establish the first Moon colony. The MFSSS, i.e. the McConaughey Foundation for Sweet Sweet Science, has pioneered spacefaring initiatives ever since." Ross switched back to his normal voice and up-nodded. "Alright."

"Wow. Just, wow."

"Wow, *alright*."

"So what's with the *alright*? Is it a decree or something?"

"Decree, alright? No, it's just a sign of respect, alright. You know that, alright."

"Assume I don't."

Ross glanced over at nothing in particular, as if to say *this guy* to someone. "One alright follows general statements, alright. Two alrights follow praise or exclamations, alright alright. Use three alrights to honor the great McConaughey directly, alright alright alright."

Max chuckled and shook his head, as if trapped by the latest conspiracy theory. "What about *four* alrights?" he said in a mocking tone.

Ross narrowed his eyes. "*Never* use four alrights. Don't even *mention* four alrights, you contemptuous douchebag."

"Whoa, my mistake," Max said, raising his hands.

Ross jumped down from the bed and trotted out of the room, lobbing a stink eye at Max as he passed. Max lifted from the bed and shuffled over to the opposite wall. A limp tap opened a cubby with a washbasin and various hygiene products. After several minutes of sprucing and grooming, he tapped a series of commands into the control panel. LEDs brightened to a pleasant hue, bed sheets disappeared into a wall slot, and a drawer full of pressed garments slid open at his waist. He slipped into a set of clean clothes, nudged the drawer closed, and turned to leave.

Max entered a cargo bay filled with belly laughs. Zoey, Perra, Ross, and Steve sat in a circle around some storage crates. Zoey stood with her back to Max, her hand covering a taut and teary face. Perra doubled over atop a cargo crate, wheezing in laughter with her arms crossing her stomach. Ross chuckled as he bounced his gaze around the group. Steve rolled around the floor, cluck-laughing and shedding feathers with each toss. Ross caught Max's confused gaze and stopped laughing. A quick *ahem* hooked the attention of everyone else. They traded cackles for sheepish demeanors as they glanced over to Max.

"What the hell was that all about?" Max said.

"Oh nothing," Zoey said. "... crab licker."

The group burst into laughter again.

Ross wiped his watering eyes. "I told them that story of, uh ... you know, alright."

Max raised an eyebrow and shrugged.

Perra slowed to a giggle. "Poor little Earthling."

"Great," Max said under his breath. "Not even privy to my own humiliations." He shook it off and shuffled towards the group. "So where are we going?"

Zoey took a needed breath, regaining some composure. "We're on our way to Phil's Place."

"A bar?" Max said.

"No, it's a planet."

"Who names a planet Phil's Place?"

"I thought that would be obvious."

Max opened his mouth to respond, then clamped it shut in frustration.

"Phil is the only inhabitant," Perra said. "Suffice to say, it's his place. He lived there alone for billions of years, then discovered he wasn't alone. It's a long story, but let's just say that he's incredibly fond of visitors. It takes a certain grace to, um, tolerate his enthusiasm."

"He is widely regarded as the most intelligent being in the universe," Zoey said. "Every now and then, we need his insight."

"And he's cool with that?" Max said, taking a seat.

"That's where the tolerance comes in," Perra said. "Most beings can't handle him."

"What, does he probe you or something?"

Zoey shifted her grin. "In a way."

Max closed his eyes and dropped his head.

"Don't worry," Perra said. "It's all copacetic. We know how to deal with him. Just don't be alarmed if he takes a keen interest in your presence."

Max responded with a limp nod.

"We're about half a poch out," Zoey said, addressing the group. "Two more jumps should do it."

"The drive should be ready for the next," Perra said.

"Gravy. Let's get to it then."

Perra lifted from the crate and hooked Zoey's waistband as they made their way to the cockpit. Steve flapped some feathers loose and pecked at a dangling latch. Ross plopped onto the floor and started grooming his belly. Max sighed, lifted from his seat, and plodded to the rear of the cargo bay for some breakfast.

CHAPTER 5

The crimson ensemble munched and slurped around the large conference table. Crumpled napkins and paper cups littered the surface, like a chaotic family outing at a fast-food restaurant. Sconces glowed at peak illumination, replacing the darkened menace with the casual grumblings of snack time. A hologram star map floated above the table with a blue arrow blinking across it. A dotted red line estimated its trajectory.

"Looks like they're headed to Phil's Place," Jerry said with a half-eaten donut in hand.

The table erupted with sighs and grumbles.

"Ugh, that guy," Carl said, drooping his eyestalks.

"Can we intercept?" Yerba said with one mouth while slurping her tasty beverage with the other.

"Perhaps," Fio said. His pudgy fingers rapped upon the table surface.

Jerry tapped his third chin, then swiped the hologram away with a noodly arm. "Here's an idea. Why don't we just snatch the Earthman with a focused teleport? If you can grab my fat ass, why not him?"

"Impossible," Gorp said. His guttural voice and hissing lisp showered saliva onto the table. "We cannot ensnare a moving target. The teleporter needs locked coordinates and time to latch."

"Can we just swipe the entire ship?" Yerba said.

Gorp tilted his head. "And how is that any different?"

Yerba shrugged tiny shoulders that barely conveyed the act of shrugging.

"Hmm," Fio said. "Given the situation, we may need to call upon the Viscid Avenger."

Jerry groaned and flopped back into his chair. "Oh for fuck's sake, Fio. How hard is it to say that it's Frank's turn?"

Frank perked up, or at least five of his eight eyes did. A slender tongue shot out of his mouth and hooked the straw of his drink.

Fio huffed and tossed his arms into the air. "Dammit, Jerry! What is it with you and all this needless balking? You are part of the Suth'ra High Council! Act like it!"

Jerry sighed. "We're all Suth'ra, Fio. That doesn't mean we have to act like conceited pricks with druid complexes."

Yerba nodded.

Gorp grunted.

Carl twisted an eyestalk. "What's a druid?"

Fio grumbled with aggravation. "Fine! Frank, suit up."

The sudden attention caused Frank to topple his drink, spilling a puddle of purple ooze across the table. He righted the cup with one of several clawed appendages and glanced around the room in embarrassment.

Fio plunked his head on the table.

"Cleanbot," Yerba said with a stern voice.

A small hover droid shot into the room with a dirty rag and spray bottle. Its spidery frame landed upon the table, surveyed the mess, then slumped its body as if to emit a sigh of annoyance. It chirped and groused under its mechanical breath as it spritzed the surface and started wiping the table clean.

Frank lifted from his seat, allowing his crimson cloak to drape from a shoulderless physique. A pair of scrawny legs supported a lumpy mass, like a wad of gum on toothpicks. Four spindly arms hung from a hairless torso with bat-like claws at the ends. All eight of his eyes focused on Fio and awaited instruction.

Fio narrowed his eyes and nodded. "You know what to do."

Frank stood motionless. Four of his eyes glanced around the room. "Um ... refresh me."

Kaeli facepalmed herself.

Fio grabbed a bagel chunk from the grips of the cleanbot and flung it at Frank. The morsel whizzed by his head and hit the wall, showering Frank with crumbs. The droid's big red eye shot up to Fio as if to curse his mother. Frank raised three of his eyebrows.

"You're the Viscid Avenger for Tim's sake! You've been sitting at this table since the meeting began. What the hell have you been doing?"

Frank cleared his throat. "To be perfectly honest, I tuned out a while ago. I've been musing on a new crepe recipe."

Jerry perked up.

Fio sustained his murder-death-kill stare. "Earthman ... Phil's Place ... intercept."

Frank saluted with a random claw. "Right. On it." He turned for the door and skittered out of the room.

Gorp coughed up a loogie that arched through the air and splatted the table near the cleanbot. The startled droid threw down its rag, flipped a pair of tiny metal birds, waved them around the group, then flew away.

* * *

Phil's Place floated inside a brilliant purple nebula out in open space. The planet orbited a red dwarf star named Phil's Shiny. Not the most inspired of names, but it's not like Phil had much choice. The star had departed its original galaxy long before Phil gained self-awareness. The galaxy may have been named Phil's Swirly had it not collided with another galaxy. Well, "collided" would be a misnomer since galaxies can pass through each other with relative ease. The billions of stars inside zip by one another without so much as a kind hello, like a fly in Texas passing another fly in Texas, with no other flies in Texas. In other words, there is a metric shit-ton of empty space between stars in galaxies.

Phil's Shiny was the unfortunate victim of a gravitational tug-of-war. Instead of drifting through unscathed, it passed between two black holes and got slingshotted out into open space. Phil didn't know that at the time because he was too busy contemplating uses for spurs on his hind fins. The lone star and its single planet floated out into the big empty. As time passed, the dots in the night sky clumped into swirling flowers, then became dots themselves. A million years later, the sky turned a pleasant shade of magenta as the lonely planet plunged into a thick nebula. The dots disappeared, leaving Phil to ponder any existential crisis alone. Not that he minded. At the time, he was slithering onto land to test out some newfound lung capacity.

The tug of forming stars slowed Phil's Shiny to a stop, enough to keep it floating around the nebula as a wandering satellite. For the next billion years, Phil continued to evolve under a blanket of purple sky, oblivious to the wonders of a universe out of reach. The churning cloud of gas and dust cloaked the planet from the prying eyes of the cosmos. That is, until Phil started talking.

These days, most ships traveled around the giant nebula like a middle-class family avoiding the ghetto. Phil always projected his "Free Hugs" invitation, prompting vessels to jump into hyperspace for a destination of anywhere else. Some vessels have unwittingly slammed into asteroid fields in the galactic equivalent of avoiding eye contact. Luckily, Zoey and Perra knew how to handle Phil and actually grew to appreciate his company. They enjoyed their wacky trysts into the purple cloud of questionable advances.

* * *

The tiny freighter ship exited hyperspace just outside of the nebula. Zoey steadied their trajectory as Perra tapped across the control panel, cooling the drives. Moments later, the hailing system went wholesale bonkers. Speakers blared, lights flashed, everything electric barked and buzzed. Zoey shook her head and punched a coms link overhead.

"Phil, calm the fuck down!"

The chaos ceased, leaving an awkward silence.

"Sorry," Phil said through the intercom, his voice soft and sheepish.

"It's okay, buddy," Perra said. "We're looking forward to seeing you."

Zoey smirked. "We even brought a few new friends."

The hailing system resumed its unhinged insanity.

Perra facepalmed herself. "Helping or hurting, sweetie?"

"New touchies! New touchies!" Phil gasped between the exclamations. "Intimate touching! Skin pleasure!"

Zoey glanced back to find a wide-eyed Max gawking at the intercom.

"It's okay," Zoey said with a chuckle. "He's harmless, I promise."

Max lowered a twitching eye to Perra. "Is she for real?" He pointed at the nebula in the viewport. "That clown-faced smog bank may as well have 'free popsicles in the basement' painted on the side."

"Don't worry," Perra said. "We know what we're doing. You'll be fine."

Zoey snickered.

Ross sauntered into the cockpit. "Alright alright. We at the grabby blob yet?"

Max cupped his hands over his face and groaned with clear exacerbation.

"Hey Phil," Zoey said in a commanding tone.

"Yes?"

"Are you going to behave yourself?"

Phil thought for a moment. "Yes?" he said, emphasizing the question.

"Good boy," Zoey said, then smirked at Max.

Max rolled his eyes and grumbled back to the cargo bay.

"Okay then," Perra said. "Phil, where's your rock these days? Drop us some digits."

"Oh yes, let's see, um ... 413-743-H3-101."

Zoey input the data. "Got it."

The console crunched the coordinates and projected a hologram map of the nebula. A glowing orange path angled around a budding star system full of comets and asteroids. Perra tapped the arch, spun the hologram, and zoomed into the detour.

"The path is clean, but we have to jump around a stellar nursery. We'll be there in a quarter poch. Sound good?"

"Mmm, yes," Phil said in a sultry voice. "Please hurry. My husk aches for embrace."

Ross cringed and recoiled. "Wow. That was unsettling, even for me."

Perra glanced down at Ross. "No *alright?*"

Ross maintained a wary stare out the viewport. "I will not besmirch the great McConaughey name by linking it to a touch-happy beanbag."

"Well," Zoey said, "that beanbag *is* the smartest being in the universe."

"He could be the reconstituted brain matter of Einstein, Sagan, and Clarence the Wonder Llama. I still wouldn't visit his house on Halloween."

"Hallo-what?"

"It's an Earth holiday where you dress up in costumes and beg strangers for candy."

Perra raised an eyebrow. "And you think *Phil* is creepy?"

Ross paused for thought. "Touché."

"How long to the next jump?" Zoey said to Perra.

Perra consulted the console. "About three c-marks. That last one was a doozy, core needs to cool a bit."

"Gravy. Good time to grab some grub."

"I second that."

They unbuckled from their seats and exited the cockpit. Ross, his gaze still affixed to the nebula, shivered the angst from his spine and followed them. Back in the cargo bay, Max munched on a fuzzy yellow veggie and sipped coffee from his favorite mug, a colorful monstrosity he found in a moonbase strip mall. Steve perched on the edge of an open food crate, studying each item with random neck jerks. He leaned forward to peck at a mystery piece, then fell inside.

"Bacock!"

"Dumb bird," Max said with a mouthful of crunch.

Steve popped his head above the crate. "Ahem, I have only been a snoodlecock for less than a poch. I'd appreciate some latitude."

"You're a chicken, dude. How hard is it to master?"

Steve fanned his wings. "Who's got two thumbs and is learning to snoodlecock? I'd point to myself, but I ain't got no goddamn thumbs."

"Says the winged cuisine."

Steve gasped and leapt from the crate. He bounded off the ledge and rage-flapped towards Max, clucking at the top of his lungs. Max yelped and scampered around the cargo bay with Steve flailing behind, pecking at anything he dared open to assault. He tripped over a chair and tumbled to the floor, allowing Steve to flutter on top and scratch his way to victory. Shooing arms tried to thwart the attack, but Steve's nimble beak found ears, cheeks, and clumps of hair.

"Hey hey hey!" Zoey said as she entered the cargo bay.

The scuffle came to an abrupt stop with Steve perched atop Max's head.

"What the hell are you guys doing?"

"A friendly fracas among civilized chaps," Steve said, then pecked Max's ear one last time, drawing a yelp before flapping to a nearby crate.

Max glared at Steve and scooped his yellow veggie from the floor.

Perra nabbed a pre-made sandwich from the crate and tossed another to Zoey, who snatched it out of the air like a seasoned shortstop. Steve jerked his gaze between them as they unwrapped their lunches and munched to satiation. Falling bread crumbs caught his attention. He flapped over to the floor next to Perra, pecked the tiny morsels, then eyed her with the pitiful gaze of a family dog. Perra smirked and broke off a piece of her sandwich.

"Here," she said and placed it on the floor.

"My deepest gratitude, kind miss," Steve said, then tore the chunk to shreds, like a weed-whacker hitting a plump croissant. Scraps of meat and bread flung through the air. Steve chirped and chased after each wayward bit.

Max lifted to his feet and dusted himself off with a few hand swipes. Examining his half-eaten veggie, he frowned at the grease stains and tossed it into a nearby waste bin. Steve perked at the sight, hopped over to the bin, flapped inside, and started devouring the veggie with extreme prejudice. The bin clanked upon the floor as Steve ravaged the helpless produce. Max shook his head and returned to the food crate for another item. He grabbed a baggie of trail mix and took a seat on a nearby crate.

"So why can't we just jump straight to Phil's Place?"

"Too dangerous," Perra said. "The nebula is very active, hot-charged if you will. Lots of new stars forming, lots of meandering asteroids and such. It's best to jump to the outer rim and consult with Phil directly. His planet is a rogue rock orbiting a roaming star."

"Let me guess," Max said with a sarcastic tone. "Phil's Shiny?"

Perra glanced to Zoey, then back to Max. "Yes, actually."

"Hardy har, make fun of the Earthling."

Ross sighed.

The waste bin fell over and clattered, startling the group. Steve spilled onto the floor with trash clinging to his body. He clucked, shook the refuse from his feathers, and waddled over to the group.

"Hey Phil," Zoey said, glancing up to the ceiling.

An overhead speaker broke with static. "Yes?"

"What do you call your star?"

"Shiiiiiiny. My precious shiny, bringer of light and skin warmth. Phil's Shiny."

Max lowered to a whisper. "He's still listening?"

"He's a telepath, doofus. Furthermore, whispering isn't going to hide anything. It's not like he's chilling in the next room."

"So he can hear everything we say?"

"Yup." Zoey finished the last bite of her sandwich. "Can hear most of your thoughts too."

Stunned into silence, Max glanced around the room in obvious discomfort. "But, what if he overhears, something, um ... unsavory?"

"Don't worry," Perra said with a polite chuckle. "Phil is well aware of his demeanor. You're not going to hurt his feelings. Just be yourself, think your thoughts, and don't fret about it."

"Hey Phil," Zoey said.

"Yes?"

"You look like a giant scabby scrotum."

"An accurate assessment, yes."

"And your freaky behavior upsets people."

"All the time, yes."

"And what is Max thinking right now?"

"He's being chased by a giant scrotum with googly eyes and out-stretched fingers."

Ross and Steve met eyes and burst into laughter.

Perra finished off her sandwich, crumpled the wrapper, and mo-seyed over to the toppled waste bin. She righted it, gathered the wayward trash, and added her wrapper to the pile. As she turned away, an intrigued Steve hopped back over to the bin and leapt in-side. Perra sighed and shook her head, opting to ignore the thwarted effort. She stepped over to a sullen Max and bumped his shoulder. "Like I said, no need to worry. You'll be fine, I promise." She winked, then turned to address the group. "I'll be in the cockpit prepping for the next jump."

"Thank you, sweetie," Zoey said. She scanned the food crate, plucked a bottle of cloudy liquid, and strolled over to the main cabin. "Gonna grab some shuteye, wake me if you need anything."

"Will do," Perra said as she disappeared up the narrow passage.

Zoey paused inside the doorway and turned back to the group. "You all should do the same. The nebula can be a bit unsettling once inside."

"How so?" Max said.

Zoey smirked. "Just get some sleep." She stepped inside and the door slid shut.

The cockpit console chirped in the distance. The hum of idle engines filled the cargo bay. Steve poked his head from the waste bin and clucked to break the silence. Max and Ross traded restive glances.

"So," Phil said. "Do you like Twister?"

Max groaned and bowed his head.

CHAPTER 6

Inside the purple nebula, a black stealth ship blinked out of hyper-space. The round vessel floated through a pocket of dust, swirling ribbons in its wake. Its glowing red viewport bathed nearby clouds in a bloody sheen. From afar, the ship resembled a black hole punched through a magenta sheet. For once, it stuck out as an anomalous presence, but not for long. The exterior flickered and faded as cloaking tech bent light particles around the frame, leaving a sliver of warped space.

Inside, the Viscid Avenger, a.k.a. Frank, tapped three of his claws across the console. The fourth nabbed a thermos of coffee and tossed a sip down his gullet. Interference from the hyperactive nebula caused circuits to blip and crackle. Frank grumbled some curses and slammed a claw onto the panel. The console belched in response, flashed the exterior, then corrected itself. Random surges and glitches continued to wreak havoc, forcing Frank to abandon the cloaking tech in favor of basic hiding. He pieced together a hologram map of the immediate vicinity. Four of his eight eyes narrowed to inspect the area. After a quick swipe and scan, he selected a small asteroid field nearby as an optimal ambush point. He locked the coordinates, took another sip of coffee, and thrust the round vessel towards the rocks.

The ship veered around the asteroids like a slalom skier owning a downhill. Frank halted his path in front of a large rock with plenty of open fissures to hide within. He pushed forward at a steady pace and slowed to a stop once inside a cozy cubby. Magnetic grips spun the ship until it faced out into the nebula. Frank killed the drive and powered down to an idle state. The glowing viewport faded into nothingness, leaving the darkened ship tucked inside the asteroid, just a small rock inside a bigger rock.

Frank sighed, grabbed a frayed book, and unzipped his form-fitting pilot suit. Form-fitting in the sense that Frank had a form and the suit kind of fit. Frank was a Gurbalurb, a species known for its hodgepodge take on evolution. When it came to random mutation, everything was on the table. No eyes, ten eyes, skin, scales, claws, fingers, bucktoothed kneecaps with hairy tongues, whatever. In fact, their only common trait was a taffy-like torso from which everything else sprouted. Furthermore, the species was hermaphroditic, meaning that any individual could be a mother or father. This made copulation a wee bit stressful since mating pairs had no clue how to satisfy each other. For most couples, sexy time meant "giving it a go" and seeing what happens. A rub here, a poke there, licks, punches, whatever tickled a fancy. More often than not, mothers had no idea they were even pregnant (or that they were mothers for that matter) until a random creature sprouted from their torso and ran away.

Young Frank had enjoyed a quiet life as an only sprout. His mother and father were asexual for the most part and never planned to procreate. He was a happy accident, the likely result of an over-packed elevator. One day, his parents awoke to find a wad of wiggling flesh in their bed that kind of resembled themselves. After closer inspection, they came to the inescapable conclusion that they were new yet slightly baffled parents. Frank traded glances with the two lumpy creatures he now shared a space with. He expelled his first sigh, unimpressed with life from day one. His parents didn't like kids all that much and he felt the same way about them. But, they got along just fine and lived together as agreeable acquaintances.

Frank spent most of his childhood in a repurposed bathroom full of bookshelves. Food was portable, but toilets were not, so his logic-driven brain decided that bathrooms were the place to be. He stocked cabinets with basic food stores and drank from the faucet when needed. Most of his waking time involved long reading sessions while pacing around his tiny personal space. He spent months at a time locked away inside his plumbed fortress, only venturing out to verify the world still existed (and to restock snacks). One day, after scratching a mental itch about flora reproduction, Frank discovered the magical realm of interstellar botany. A keen interest morphed into a mild obsession, then exploded into a major psychological bender.

Frank abandoned the toilet and dove into his newfound fetish. Before long, he amassed an impressive collection of medicinal plants from all around the galaxy. His obsessive analysis and fruitful experiments turned him into a revered botanist, even before his legal drinking age. (He could grow and use hallucinogenic terror blossoms, but a relaxing sip of ethanol was somehow illegal.) His astounding achievements caught the attention of stuffy academics, pharma companies, and eventually, the Suth'ra Society.

While developing a cross-strain of chocolate and coffee (which he dubbed "choffee"), Frank received a mysterious message from an unknown source. His vast knowledge of taxonomy and Sudoku allowed him to decipher the location of a roaming Suth'ra mega-vessel. At the time, a team of Suth'ra botanists were struggling to perfect a recipe for hot sauce (the never-ending quest to find a perfect heat-flavor ratio). And so, they forwarded Frank an invitation. Frank decoded, accepted, and joined the Suth'ra Society with two lifelong missions. One, solve the heat-flavor ratio once and for all, and two, cure cancer. In that order.

As of today, he had yet to solve the first. But at least he got to wear a cool space suit and stalk an Earthling through a kick-ass nebula.

* * *

A tiny freighter ship exited hyperspace just outside the asteroid field, prompting a beacon scanner to bark inside the stealth vessel. Frank marked a stopping place in his trashy romance novel and set it aside. A slender arm reached across the console and muted the scanner. Seven eyes narrowed as he scrutinized the freighter in the distance.

"Diagnostic," he said.

"M-class freighter," the ship said, using the robotic voice of an 80's arcade game. "Heavily armed, four and a half life forms inside."

Frank lifted three of his eyebrows. "Half?"

"Cyborg feline."

"Oh." Frank shifted his lips, then shook it off. "Establish a comlink to Fio."

"Who?"

He glanced at the intercom. "Fio."

"Who?"

"Oh for Tim's sake, call Fio!"

"Who?"

Frank huffed and rubbed his forehead. "His Impeccable Majesty, Grandmaster Fiolandon, High Lord of the Suth'ra Council, Speaker of Truth, Defender of Reason."

"Right away, sir."

The hologram projector crackled with static, then pieced together the robed bust of Fio.

"Silence!" Fio said. "The valiant Viscid Avenger beckons the High Council."

Frank blinked five eyes, then rolled the other three.

"Report."

"Target acquired. Shall I engage?"

Fio stroked his plump chin. "Your Shawl of Invisibility is down. Why is this so?"

"It's cloak tech, Fio. No need for the wizard-speak."

"Insolence!" Fio slammed a fist onto the table. "You shall rue the day you disrespect the High Lord of the Council!"

Frank glanced away and shook his head. "Do you hear yourself right now?"

"Frank has a point," Kaeli said from afar. "You sound like a douchebag dungeon master."

"Insolence!" Fio pointed off-hologram, cropping the tip of his finger.

A chair squeaked. "I'm getting some coffee," Kaeli said. "Anybody want some?" Mumbles responded, followed by footsteps and a door slam.

Fio dropped his arm, folded his fingers, and cleared his throat. "Report."

"We just did this," Frank said, spreading all four arms.

Fio remained still, clinging to a nonexistent menace.

Frank sighed. "Target acquired. Shall I engage?"

Fio re-stroked his plump chin. "Hmm ... no, too risky. The Omen is a seasoned fighter pilot and would likely crush your feeble attempt."

Frank rolled all eight eyes. "Okay, so now what?"

Fio paused for thought. "I see you have freed yourself of your suit."

"A necessary action. It was hot and itchy."

"See?" Jerry said from a distance.

"Shut up, Jerry!" Fio said, pointing another rigid finger off-hologram.

"Have you ever worn one of those sweaty trash bags? I couldn't feel my giblets after 20 ticks. It's a dumb, moronic, stupidly stupid design."

"You're stupid," Fio said in a passive-aggressive tone.

Jerry stood from his chair, prompting Fio to stand from his. The pair barked insults at each other in a whirlwind of gibberish. Frank grabbed his romance novel and resumed where he had left off. Fio stomped away from the hologram visual, leaving a swiveling chair in his wake. After a bout of off-hologram drama, Fio returned to his seat, gasping and panting with his hood tossed back. Frank glanced up from his book as Fio blotted his scalp, took a needed breath, and tried to rekindle any semblance of order.

"Anyhoo," Fio said, tossing Jerry a sour glance. "Follow the target. Wait for an appropriate time to intercept on the surface of Phil's Place."

Frank slapped his book shut. "Oh c'mon! You're going to make me go down there and deal with that loony?"

Fio waved off the concern. "Stop being so dramatic. Phil is harmless."

Frank narrowed four of his eyes. "*Harmless?* If memory serves, Gorp went through two years of intense therapy after a scouting visit."

Fio glanced over to a shaking Gorp, who held up three fingers.

"You'll be fine," Fio said, then killed the transmission.

Frank applied three facepalms and barked an array of unsavory insults. He plunked a claw onto the console and mumble-pouted while prepping the ship for pursuit.

* * *

Inside the tiny freighter, Max stared at his own reflection with slack-jawed fascination. There it was, plain as day, his own brain floating behind his eyeballs. He had awoken with transparent skin and bones, a tweak abundantly apparent even before opening his eyelids. Twisting his head from side to side, he poked at his noggin like a jellyfish on the beach. Everything felt normal. Skin was smooth, bones were hard, tongue was dry from prolonged jaw dangling. All muscles and organs were appropriate colors, just faded to the point of transparency.

Ross, also transparent, stared at Max from the bed. His ears remained cocked backwards in concern, not that anyone could tell. His innards churned in silence like a well-oiled machine, which, in reality, he was. Tiny gears and pistons shifted with every motion, creating the wet dream of any steampunk fanatic. A pair of mechanical eyeballs glanced around the room. He sighed, shook his head, and returned his gaze to Max.

"You've been staring at yourself for an uncomfortably long time now. What's wrong?"

Max swayed his hands in front of the mirror, creating a ripple effect. "Dude, I look like a study doll for a science classroom."

Ross lifted an invisible eyebrow.

Max pressed a palm to his abdomen and chuckled like an idiot as his organs shifted from side to side. "It's like having a cheat sheet for med school."

Everything non-biological (and non-cyborg) remained solid and opaque. The walls remained dull and gray. The control panels remained smooth and black. White sheets and a brown blanket rested atop a tarnished bed frame. The solid gray door slid open, prompting Max to yelp and fumble for clothes. He tapped the wall panel for the laundry drawer, which shot out with nothing inside. A swift hand yanked a sheet from the bed and wrapped it around his waist.

"What's the matter?" Perra said from the doorway. She stood with her arms crossed, also transparent, also naked. Her muscles and organs twisted over each other in peculiar arrangements. A pair of purple hearts beat at her side like elevated kidneys. Her stomach, liver, and various intestines filled the central cavity. A spleen-like organ pulsated below the mass, causing Max to question his biological acumen.

Max looked her up and down, then back to the drawer, then back to Perra. "What happened to my clothes?"

"Your what?"

"My, um ..." Max turned to Ross, who had exited the conversation in favor of grooming his transparent thigh. Returning his attention to Perra, his teenage brain blurted out the most pressing observation. "You're naked."

Perra glanced down at her chest. "Yeah, so?"

Max had always dreamed of an attractive naked woman walking into his bedroom on purpose, but the nature of the situation had sucked all sexual tension out of the air. There they were, exposed breasts filled with fatty tissue and blood vessels, and yet, any sense of arousal seemed as distant as the next star system. An odd sense of liberation washed over him. He took a deep breath, dropped the sheet, and stood proud in his glassy birthday suit.

"Now you're naked," Ross said, feeling the need to prod the predicament.

Max's anxieties flooded back, like a rampaging army of naked-in-school nightmares. He cupped his crotch, not that it mattered, and fumbled for the sheet.

Perra rolled her eyes. "Anyway, jump is complete, one more to Phil's Place. We'll execute after cooldown, no more than a c-mark or two. In the meantime, there's a stunning stellar nursery just outside, thought you would like to take a gander."

"Thanks," Max said, still clinging to the sheet around his waist. "Although, I'm pretty sure I'll need a nap before we get to Phil's Place."

"Why?"

Max glanced back and forth between pellucid Perra and steampunk Ross. "No reason."

"Suit yourself," Perra said, then turned to leave.

Max eyed her pristine butt as she exited the room, again unmoved. The door slid shut, leaving Max to his needless modesty. He took a deep breath, then another, and another, watching lungs inflate inside a glossy chest. Lowering to the bed, he stretched away the awkwardness and turned to the rear wall.

"Fikarek."

The surface faded to reveal a massive cloud of gas and dust with a cluster of brilliant orbs peppering the interior. Widened eyes wandered around the forging star system. It bloomed with every color of the rainbow, turning his body into a fleshy prism. Every movement twisted beams of color around the cabin. Max giggled at the newfound party trick, tossing ribbons of light with his open palms.

Ross glanced up from an extended thigh. "You really are just a simple wanker."

"Shut up, gearface."

"That's racist."

Max bent a beam into Ross's eyes, causing him to grunt and recoil.

For the next several hours, Max continued his curious examination, like a clever chimp with a hand mirror. Eating and drinking provided an endless source of entertainment, as did the eventual expulsion. He traced nerve strands and blood vessels like a kid playing a rousing game of connect the dots. A brief bout of calisthenics taught him more about muscle movement than all of his biology classes combined. His inquiry peaked at wondering what sex would be like with a transparent partner. The resulting arousal made him appreciate just how fast blood moved where it needed to.

*   *   *

The freighter floated in a pocket of empty space inside the purple nebula. Budding stars and glowing gas twinkled overhead, creating the spacefaring equivalent of a Pink Floyd laser light show. Inside, a pair of transparent naked Mulgawats prepared the ship for jump. Their human cohort had taken the opportunity to catch a strategic nap.

An asteroid bank drifted nearby, shrouding Frank and his stealthy sphere. Inside, a hologram panel of target data scrolled atop the console, bathing his bored expression in a golden sheen. Flickers of light zigzagged through his glassy body, as if bewildered by the mishmash of mystery organs. The occasional ping of refresh sliced through the deafening silence. One eye read the readout while five eyes watched the ship in the distance. The other two continued reading the trashy romance novel off to the side. His jaw dropped open as all eight eyes widened and refocused on the novel. "Wow. Bargomeck does know how to write a good flimflarb."

The main engines ignited behind the freighter, hooking Frank's attention. He marked a stopping point and set the novel aside. The ship pitched a bit, then disappeared into a sliver of purple light. Frank gripped the control yoke with all four claws and thrust the stealth ship out of the fissure. He powered the magnetic drive and slithered through the asteroid field. Sailing past a final rock, he input the stolen coordinates and thumped the jump icon. The ship hummed for a tick, then followed the freighter into hyperspace.

Moments later, a dark triangular ship detached from a nearby asteroid and thrust into open space. It locked onto the same coordinates and jumped.

CHAPTER 7

A barrage of shrieks and sirens yanked Max from a cozy snooze. Muffled curses from the cockpit calmed the ruckus, likely Zoey berating Phil upon arrival. Max lifted his arms for a brief inspection and welcomed the return of an opaque epidermis. But unbeknownst to him, pine trees were now deciduous. Ross lifted from a furry pile at the base of the bed and wandered up to Max's chest, making sure to step on his crotch along the way (a reliable yelp button). He headbutted Max in the chin and launched into a throaty purr.

"Yes, ugh, hello," Max said, dodging the intrusion.

Ross continued his persistent morning ritual.

After several knocks and a mouthful of fur, Max cupped his companion's face with both hands. "That's enough. I'm up, you can stop."

Ross quieted and scrunched his brow. "You know, now that I think about it, I'm not sure why I even do this. I don't eat, I'm not hungry, so it serves no purpose."

"Compulsion, maybe?"

"Yeah, like when I see an open box and *need* to be inside it. And I mean *neeeed*, like a sexual yearning or something."

Max nudged Ross off his chest. "And on that note, I'm definitely up."

Tossing the sheets aside, he swung his legs out of bed and dropped his feet to the cold floor. A moaning yawn and reaching stretch greeted the new day, but then he slouched with the realization of what lay ahead. Lifting from the bed, he shuffled over to the wall panel and thumped it with his forehead, opening the sink cubby. He wallowed through a grooming routine, complete with bitchy groans and petty sighs. Subsequent taps reset the sink and opened a laundry drawer. He slipped into a fresh set of duds, accenting each yank and pull with a catty grunt. A final tap and slap reset the room and opened the door.

"Bacock!" Steve said from just outside.

Max flinched into a stumble. "Ugh, jeez, warn me next time."

"I submit that *was* an appropriate warning."

"He means *don't stand outside the door like a serial killer.*" Ross trotted into the cargo bay. A tail whip smacked Steve in the face, causing him to flap and jerk away.

"Puss."

"Cock."

Ross hissed.

Steve growled, which caught everyone off guard.

"Children!" Zoey said from the cockpit. "Stow your shit and come check this out."

Max clanked up the narrow passage with Ross and Steve plodding behind. Ross leapt into Perra's lap as Steve flapped up to Zoey's headrest. Two jaws and a beak dropped when they caught the image in the viewport. The massive horizon of Phil's Place stretched from end to end, its vast blue seas reflecting sunlight through a crystal clear atmosphere. The mocha browns of towering mountain ranges carved through sheets of green. Thin ribbons of white clouds cast shadowy strips along the surface. And then the plat du jour, a colossal band of icy rings lifted from below and encircled the entire planet. They glittered with a garnet hue, reflecting the red dwarf star in the distance.

"That is the second most beautiful thing my eyes have ever seen," Steve said through a bewitched expression.

"What was the first?" Zoey said.

"A canocrab fishing for finnelworms off the ivory coast of Hanwark during the second winter solstice."

"That's oddly specific," Max said.

"I wouldn't expect an Earthling to understand."

"And that's oddly prickish."

Steve narrowed his eyes and slogged them over to Max. "Is your entire species just one big twit brigade or is it just you?"

Everyone started to respond, but Max injected a waving finger. "Na na na na no, all of you just shut up. You can all dump on the Earthling later. Right now I'm more concerned with Huggy McSackerton down there."

"Ooo, he means me!" Phil said through the intercom, thrilled to have a conversational opening. A tentacle hand sprouted from his body and shot into the air like an eager grade school student, not that anyone could see it. "Mmm, yes, huggy time."

Max sighed and dropped his chin.

Perra tried her best to hold in a snicker.

"We're in orbit, buddy," Zoey said. "Where would you like us to land?"

"38 lat, 14 long, rolling valley east of the mountain base." Phil's speedy delivery sounded like a preteen boy on a sugar high reciting his favorite ice cream flavors.

"Got it," Perra said, inputting the coordinates. "Be on the ground shortly."

A fresh barrage of flashes and sirens erupted inside the cockpit. Steve squawked and flapped behind Zoey's head, releasing a flurry of feathers. Ross hissed, because why not. Perra snorted with muffled laughter as Zoey slammed a fist onto the console.

"Dammit, Phil! Get a grip! I swear to Tim, I will turn this ship around and go right on our merry way."

The chaos ceased.

Perra covered her mouth in a feeble attempt to control her laughter.

"Sorry," Phil said like a scolded child.

"It's okay, bud." She smirked and glanced at Max. "And by the way, the Earthling *cannot wait* to meet you."

The flashes and sirens returned.

Max flailed his arms as if to shout *WTF lady?!* He huffed with as much petulance as he could muster, then stomped into the cargo bay.

* * *

On the other side of the planet, strategically out of view, a round black stealth ship floated in orbit. It listed with a slow spin, as if conked or disabled. Inside, Frank gripped his romance novel with all four claws, holding it close to his face. All eight eyes devoured every word. They refused to blink as tears streamed from five of them. After reading the last sentence of the book, he howled in agony and punched the wall. "He doesn't love you anymore, Vinka! Why did you go down there?! *Whyyyy?!*" He cradled the book to his chest and sobbed for a solid minute.

Regaining an air of composure, Frank set the book aside and stroked it like a treasured pet. "So good, so good." He sniffled, shook his head, and sighed with completion. Two claws grabbed the control yoke while the other two tapped commands into the console. The ship righted itself, at least to a noticeable degree, and aligned with the giant red rings. A hologram depiction of the planet pieced itself together above the console. Frank studied it with his three good eyes while the others recovered from weeping. "Computer, lock onto the M-class freighter and trace its trajectory down to the surface."

"Sure thing, buddy!" the computer said, channeling a car salesman that needed to meet quota. "Anything else I can do you for, pal?"

"Yes. Scan the terrain and determine an ideal landing spot for concealed interception."

"Roger dodger!"

The hologram planet spun and zoomed into a blinking red X, marking the freighter's destination. A blinking blue X appeared close by, denoting a hidden landing zone tucked behind a rocky outcrop.

The hologram recentered onto the blue X and flashed an arrow into the sky. The icon raced down to the surface and buried itself into the blue X, adding a splash of pixels to the *park here* directive. Frank balked as an animated landing strip appeared.

"That's enough, 'puter. I got the memo."

"Sorry, good buddy! I'm just so gosh darn excited to help!"

"Bring it down a notch, 'puter."

"Can do, friend-aloo! What would you like?"

"Drop the coked-up cult leader and give me something mellow, like a gothic teen."

The computer huffed in a phlegmy female voice. "This better, or something?"

"That works. Thanks, 'puter."

"Whatever."

Frank studied the hologram, tracing a glowing trajectory that hugged the mountain range and shielded his approach. He nodded with approval, then thrust the ship forward and prepped for entry. Soon after, a magnetic cocoon encased the ship as it punched through the upper atmosphere.

Tucked away inside the towering red rings, a triangular ship clung to an icy boulder. Its sleek frame and sweeping viewport reflected the warm glow of Phil's Shiny. Inside, a shadowed pilot studied the stealth ship as it sliced through the atmosphere and disappeared into a mountain pass. The hologram readout from Frank's computer floated above the console. The pilot fed the trajectory data into its navigation system and detached from the rock.

* * *

The tiny freighter sailed over a primal landscape, adding trails of white exhaust to an otherwise pristine sky. The boxy ship stuck out as an infiltrator of sorts, like an unwashed vagrant showing up for a fancy dinner. It flew over a rocky outcrop and into a wide valley full of algae ponds and sandy stone. The steep walls of mountains lifted from the far edges, trapping clouds at their peaks. The planet radiated natural beauty under a blanket of serene silence.

"There," Perra said, pointing to a slate platform near the center of the valley.

"Got it," Zoey said and swiped across the console.

Hull thrusters ignited, spilling pillars of blue flame. The landing panels slid open, allowing three tarnished claws to lower from within. The vessel rumbled above the platform, blowing dust in every direction. Landing claws gripped the surface like a practiced gecko. The main engines broke and spun down, leaving the ship to a quiet landscape.

For a moment.

Off in the distance, a dull rumble echoed through the valley. A thin cloud of dust lifted from behind a nearby hill. Before long, a fleshy boulder rolled over the top, spraying a wake of dirt like a raging powerboat. Phil careened down the hill towards the tiny ship. His anxious bellows filled the valley, like a charging army with a death wish.

The airlock slid open, revealing Zoey and Perra in their patented ass-kicking poses. Zoey filled her lungs with crisp, clean air, and expelled the same *aaaaaah* from every breath mint commercial. She grinned and dropped to the surface. Perra followed, hopping from the ship and landing with the grace of a gymnast. A nervous Max poked his head around the airlock, then crawled down to the surface like a toddler testing chair height.

Zoey lifted an arm to shield her eyes from the bright sunlight. A quick scan uncovered the emotional meat sack racing towards them a football field away. She donned a toothy smile, opened her arms wide, and skipped towards the rumbling creature. Phil skidded to a halt, wailed like a banshee, sprouted a dozen tentacles, wrapped them around Zoey, and sucked her into his body like a hungry octopus. Perra giggled as Phil pulsated with unbridled joy. Max wore an expression of utter horror.

"Holy goose fuck," Max said. "That thing just ate Zoey!"

"No, she's fine," Perra said with a polite chuckle. "That's just how he says hello."

Max covered his mouth with both hands, fighting the urge to vomit. Ross leapt from the ship and landed as every cat does, in total silence like a furry ninja. He moseyed out from behind Max's legs, caught a glimpse of the vibrating flesh pillow, and poofed with fright.

"Sweet mercy on a pogo stick, is that Phil?"

"No, it's his half-sister Alice." Perra rolled her eyes. "Did you seriously just ask that question?"

"I, um ... uh ..." His positronic brain refused to conjure a witty retort. He just stood there, poofed and gawking at the bouncy monstrosity.

"Bacock!" Steve said from the airlock, then flapped his way towards the blob. He landed atop the mass and jerked his head from side to side with intense fascination. Sharp talons gripped the thick hide, allowing him to ride waves of quivering blubber. He dropped his beak to the bumpy skin and started pecking between the folds.

Phil gasped. He unraveled Zoey with a fresh sheen of mucus and carefully reached for the snoodlecock as if a butterfly had landed on his nose. Steve eyed the encroaching tentacles with mounting concern. Phil shrieked like a toddler at a birthday party. "New touchie!" he said and slurped the bird into his bulk, expelling a puff of feathers.

"That's enough," Zoey said, flinging strips of slime from her fingers.

Phil extended a tentacle and pooped the snoodlecock onto the ground. Steve, also covered in mucus, trembled in the dirt as green ooze dripped from his beak. He climbed to his feet, took a measured breath, and shook his body like a dog out of the rain. Cords of slime flew everywhere. Zoey sighed as gooey impacts added to her own collection. Perra dodged the shower as best she could, but ended up with a few cringe-inducing dollops.

"Ugh," she said. "I was hoping to avoid this."

"Says the often-greasy mechanic," Zoey said.

"That's different."

"How so?"

Perra tilted her head, glanced over to Phil, then back to Zoey as if to say *are you kidding me right now?*

Phil giggled like a schoolgirl and rolled towards Perra, prompting Ross to skitter beneath the ship. Perra sighed as a tentacle wrapped around her waist and plucked her from the ground. The sphincter of another engulfed her head and gave her a slimy swirl, turning two punky ponytails into a single clumped mess. She winced and spat as Phil lowered her back to the ground.

"Ugh," Perra said, wiping her face.

"Serves you right," Zoey said with a chuckle.

Perra wrung some goo from her hair, then patted Phil's quivering hide. "It's good to see you too, buddy."

Zoey glanced around the area. "Where did Max go?"

Having witnessed the horrifying greetings of a grabby meatbag, a terrified Max had retreated to the ship and hid inside an empty cargo container. But, he forgot that Phil was a telepath, rendering a clever hiding place not so clever at all. In fact, he had unknowingly wrapped himself as a gift box. Phil, having already relayed this to the group, awaited a green light to open said gift.

Zoey gestured to the open airlock. "By all means, go get 'em."

Phil squeed. "Aaaah ha ha ha goody goody goody!" He spun towards the ship, kicking up arcs of dirt. His massive body slammed into the side of the vessel, wedging itself in the airlock. His butt, or whatever part hung from the ship, wagged so hard that it shook the hull and creaked the landing gear. Tentacles shot out from the mass, hooked the crate, and yanked it outside. Max screamed as the box sailed through the air and thumped onto the ground. Phil lifted the crate overhead, flipped the lid, and dumped out a flailing Max. His body landed on Phil like a stuntman on an airbag.

Phil froze.

Max froze.

The rest of the group traded puzzled glances.

After a long and awkward silence, Phil raised a pair of tentacles, plucked Max from atop his bulk, and gently set him on the ground. A violent shiver shook the scrotal mass before rolling over to Zoey's side. Phil sprouted a tentacle and pointed it at the Earthling. "That ... is disgusting."

Max, now standing by himself like a leper, examined his body for a heinous growth he never noticed. "What the hell are you talking about?"

Phil tensed up, forming a multi-sided dice. "Holy hell, and that *voice*. Ugh, how can you stand being on the same ship with it?"

Ross burst into laughter from behind a landing claw.

"Oh he's not that bad," Perra said, offering a social olive branch. "He helps out around the ship. We even employ him as my grease monkey protégé."

Phil gasped. "You let him in the *engine room*? I hope you have enough disinfectant. Seriously, you might want to get your ship detailed."

"Wait, wait, wait," Max said with the aid of jazz hands. "*You* ... are grossed out by *me*?"

Phil leaned over to Zoey and whispered. "Does he not see the irony in that statement?"

Ross wheezed between laughing fits.

Steve decided to peck at random pebbles.

"I thought you'd be thrilled," Zoey said to Max. "You're now immune to the entire reason why most beings in the universe avoid this planet."

Phil sprouted a few hands and started massaging Zoey's shoulders.

"Yeah, but ..." Max sulked a bit as he fought the sting of rejection. He sighed and stepped towards Phil. "Are you sure you don't want to—"

Phil jerked backwards. "Ew ew ew, keep it away!" His hulking mass grabbed Zoey and slid her between him and Max.

Max frowned, kicked a pebble, and slogged back to the ship like a pouty child. He crawled into the airlock, glanced back with puppy dog eyes, then disappeared into the cargo bay. Ross wiped his eyes and trotted out from behind the landing gear.

"Ooo!" Phil snatched the kitty with a shooting tentacle, drawing a meow-yelp. He cradled the feline to his leathery flesh like an evil mastermind hatching a plan. A collection of tiny hands sprouted from the bulk and stroked Ross from every angle. Ross locked eyes with Perra, screaming *HELP ME* under a shower of fingers.

"Anyway," Zoey said to Phil, "we're in desperate need of intel. Do you have a less exposed place where we can talk? We've been marked by an unknown party and need your help."

"Can I keep holding the kitty?" Phil said.

Ross, still eye-locked with Perra, shook his head.

"Sure," Perra said, adding a wink.

Ross clenched his furry lips.

"Tee hee!" The gaggle of hands hugged Ross in unison. "There's a hidden cave system at the base of mountains to the northeast. Big enough for your ship, kind of musky, but there's a pretty waterfall and lots of interesting rocks. Follow me and bring a flashlight." Ross yipped as Phil slurped him into his body and sped away.

Zoey chuckled and hooked Perra's hand. "Ross is never going to forgive you for that."

Perra smiled. "Probably not, but maybe it will soften his cocky attitude."

They strolled towards the ship with Steve clucking and prancing behind. Zoey hopped into airlock, offered a hand to Perra, then tromped up to the cockpit. Steve flapped into the cargo bay as the door slid shut. Thrusters ignited, lifting the ship from the rocky base. The vessel angled towards the mountains and kicked forward in pursuit.

Behind a nearby outcrop, six of Frank's eyes watched the freighter disappear over a hill.

CHAPTER 8

The tiny freighter cruised over a flawless mural, splashing ponds of algae with every bank and turn. Zoey followed Phil's tracks with relative ease, due in most part to the fact that he was the only mobile critter on the planet. He carved through the soil like a turbo tractor, leaving small channels of pressed dirt behind him. The complete lack of trees and other plant life (besides algae of course) exposed his location to any visitor with a keen eye. However, the combination of global winds and seismic activity erased his tracks on a regular basis, like a vigorous shake of an Etch A Sketch.

The vessel sailed around a bend and over a deep ravine. Phil's tracks hugged the edge before plunging down a side slope. The ship followed, floating down to a babbling river. Smooth stones of all shapes and colors peeked through the crystal-clear water, creating a kaleidoscope of rippling light. A fresh canal of dirt snaked along the river edge towards a towering waterfall in the distance. Zoey and Perra lifted widened eyes to the mountainside far above where a gaping mouth showered water from an internal river system. The viewport fogged as the ship passed into a bank of hanging mist. Zoey enabled a pair of external wipers and slowed the ship to a comfortable approach.

Just ahead, Phil pulsated at the base of the waterfall with a dampened Ross raised overhead. The cyborg feline hissed and scratched at the tentacles, causing them to jerk away and shake off the painful stings. With the ship in view, Phil slurped Ross back into his body cavity and spun through the waterfall, entering the hidden cave.

Perra tapped some commands into the console, lifting a holo-gram grid of the cave system onto the viewport. Zoey slowed the ship to a hovering creep just above the river and slipped through the cascade. Columns of water pounded the vessel, giving it a much-needed rinse. Thrusters evaporated the falling water, creating a dense fog. Perra powered the external floodlights, illuminating the massive hollow. Beams of light bounced from surface to surface, reflecting the ship's presence under a glaze of moisture. Small boulders littered a field of reddish mud. Enormous stalactites with sharp tips hung from a craggy ceiling. The engine rumble caused a few to sway in precarious manners. Perra puckered her face with mild concern as Zoey pushed forward at a cautious pace.

Phil rolled up a small incline and into a secret room at the rear of the cavern, prompting Zoey to follow. She floated the ship through a narrow passageway and into the hidden hollow. Phil occupied the center of a round cave with Ross cradled to his flesh. He sprouted a thumbs-up, to which Zoey replied and lowered the landing gear. The vessel came to a rest atop a bed of soft gravel. She killed the thrusters as Perra powered down the ship. The external lights dimmed to a conversational hue as they lifted from their seats and tromped to the cargo bay.

Max continued to pout upon a crate, his head lowered and hands folded. Thumbs twisted over one another as he struggled to come to grips with the rejection. Perra stopped in front of him and sighed.

"Why on Tim's Blue Terra are you still moping?"

Max frowned. "How would you feel if an unfussy grab bag found *you* revolting?"

Perra ran a hand through her clumpy hair and smacked his cheek with a slimy palm. "Relieved, to be honest."

Max cringed, unsure of what to be upset by the most.

"The beacon scanner picked up nothing," Zoey said as she emerged from the cockpit. "We should be clear to parle."

Perra snorted. "*Parle*? What are you, a pirate?"

"Shut up, smartass. You know what I meant."

"Just breaking your beans, let's go chat with Philly." She glanced over to Max. "You too, Earthman. Get a move on."

Max groaned with the drama of a privileged preteen and lifted from the crate. The airlock door slid open and all four dropped to the soft gravel. The muggy air coated lungs and dampened skin, making for an unpleasant romp all around. The freighter sat in idle silence, casting cones of faint light into the cavern, like street lamps in the rain. The resulting shadows created a noir vibe, minus brimmed hats and the glow of cigars. The dull roar of the waterfall in the distance shrouded the meeting from any prying ears, an ideal spot for a shady discussion.

They stepped over to Phil, making sure to settle within gossip range. Phil cradled Ross and rocked him back and forth like a newborn. Ross eyed the group through a bitter expression. He shook his head and mouthed *I hate you so much* to Perra, who smirked in response. Steve buried his head into the soft gravel for a moment, then jerked it free, flinging tiny pebbles onto Phil and everyone else. He did it again and again before Zoey grew weary and berated him. He flapped in response, freeing another batch of wayward feathers. Zoey glanced back at the tunnel entrance, took a deep breath, and returned her full attention to their bulbous friend.

"Okay, so here's the short and skinny. We stopped off at Durangoni Station for a resupply and learned from Gamon that I've been marked for assassination, presumably because I killed Halim."

"Uh huh," Phil said, still stroking Ross.

"The assassin, a gimp-suited butterball, tried to hit us at the station, but we narrowly escaped thanks to Steve, who is apparently a mind-shifter of sorts."

"Uh huh."

"We have no idea who the assassin is, who they work for, or why

I've been targeted."

"Uh huh."

"Furthermore, we have no idea who Steve is, or if there is any credibility to his story."

"Uh huh."

An inept silence fell upon the group. Zoey glanced over to Perra, who shrugged, then tossed back to Phil. She raised her brow and spread her palms.

"Oh, sorry, my turn, okay, um ..." Phil placed Ross on the ground and gave him a friendly pat. Ross remained by his side with a stiff posture and irked gaze, like the creepy translator standing next to Jabba the Hutt. Phil sprouted a pair of professorial hands to accent each point. "Okay, so, first off of all, Steve is harmless. His story is completely true. Yarnwal, mind jumper, excessively long name, every-thing. He really is just mixed up in this whole thing. He saved your lives and you owe him one."

Perra nudged Zoey. "See?"

"Thank you, kind brain pouch," Steve said, then scraped his beak through the gravel. He flapped with each pass and flung pea-sized rocks everywhere.

Perra batted away a few incomings. "Jeez, would you stop al-ready?"

Steve jerked his gaze up to Perra.

"This is an inert planet, doofus. There's nothing down there."

"Oh," Steve said, then went back to digging.

Zoey rolled her eyes.

"Secondly," Phil said. "It's not a mark for assassination. It's a mark for capture."

"*Capture*? By who?"

"By the Suth'ra Society."

Perra expelled a huff of shock.

Zoey slacked her jaw. "The Suth'ra want to *kidnap* me? Then why the hell were they shooting at us?"

"No, not *you*. They don't give two ballsacks about you ladies. They want *him*." Phil pointed at Max behind them, now gagged and bound in the arms of a sneaking Frank. Phil waved excitedly. "Hi Frank!"

Frank yipped and started sprinting towards the waterfall with Max underarm. Zoey and Perra gave immediate chase, kicking up pebbles. One of them plinked Steve in the face, drawing a cluck and flap. He watched the pair round a bend in pursuit, then went back to digging for the sheer joy of digging. Phil scooped a petrified Ross from the ground and resumed his villainous petting.

Frank skidded around a corner and into the main cavern. His lanky legs kicked up mud with every giraffe-like stride. Max squirmed beneath his arms, spewing muffled yawps and curses. Frank kept all eight eyes on the prize. The roar of the waterfall grew louder and louder with each wet stomp. His three lungs settled into a rhythm of huff, grunt, repeat. Zoey and Perra flowed into the main cavern like seasoned sprinters, gaining on him with every step. His rubbery torso twisted for a gander, then yelped at the sight of the closing Mulgawats. He kicked forward with a shot of rubagoo (the Gurbalurb equivalent of adrenaline) and tapped a comlink device attached to his ear.

"Well if it isn't the Viscid Aveng—"

"Shut the fuck up, Fio! I need a yank!"

"Status?"

"Earthman acquired, The Omen in pursuit, give me a goddamn yank!"

Fio sighed. "You don't have to be a dick about it."

Despite the predicament, Frank managed to roll three of his eyes.

"I'm on it, Frank," Jerry said. "Stand by."

Frank glanced back at his pursuers, now within spitting distance. "Ah! Hurry!"

"You're moving too fast," Jerry said. "We can't lock you for teleport. You have to stop."

"Can't stop," Frank said through heavy panting. "What about *The Omen in pursuit* did you not underst—"

A large hairy beast slammed into Frank from the side, knocking him off his feet. After a flight fit for slow-motion, Frank smacked the floor with a splash of mud. Momentum plucked Max from his grasp. He sailed through the air and thumped the ground, sliding to a stop against a boulder. He moaned in discomfort and managed to sound like a bitchy child even while bound and gagged. Frank squirmed in the muck, stunned and disoriented. Zoey and Perra glided to a stop in front of the intruder.

"Gamon!" Perra said with a toothy smile and threw her arms around him.

"Hey, fuzzball," Zoey said, punching his shoulder.

"Good to see you girls," Gamon said, adding a wink and grunt. He stomped towards a writhing Frank, lifting waves of mud with broad feet. "Tend to your friend. I'll take care of this idiot."

* * *

A checkered grid of backlit panels bathed the conference room in a harsh white light. Wall sconces flickered away as if blissfully un-aware of their superfluous presence. Silence infected the chamber like an unwelcome guest that refused to leave. Pastry crumbs littered the table, the remnants of a ravaged snack cart topped with crumpled wrappers. Filth and disarray staked permanent claims, due in large part to a pissed off cleanbot. The immense round table continued to emit an ominous glow, but lost any and all menace due to the aptly lit room and foul mood of its occupants.

Crimson robes draped from chair backs and door hooks. Fio, the only member still cloaked, sat facedown on the table with arms flopped across the surface. His labored breathing clouded the glass every few ticks. Carl slumped in his own chair with eyestalks dangling across the back. He stared at the rear wall while still facing forward, an impressive trick despite the current vibe. Yerba leaned on a yel-low-spotted elbow while rapping her talons on the table. She inhaled a deep breath into her left mouth and expelled a sputtering sigh from her right. Kaeli slumped forward in her chair and stared at the table surface through a single dejected eye. Her dangling dreadlocks hid her demoralized expression quite well. Gorp faced a rear wall, his amphibious body rocking back and forth. Each sway knocked his squishy forehead against the surface, leaving a sheen of slime. Jerry puddled atop his oversized chair, adding a few more chins to his collection. He sighed, then climbed to his feet with a wearied body language that radiated failure.

"Getting some coffee. Hands up for cups."

A silent batch of limp hands raised into the air.

Jerry nodded a count and turned for the door. "Berb."

* * *

Back inside the rear cave, Zoey and Perra stood over a bound Frank. He sat atop a small boulder with all four claws tied behind his back. His lanky legs, also bound, rocked back and forth in anxious boredom. Three eyes maintained their miffed stares at the Mulgawats while the other five surveyed the cavern.

Max sat atop another small boulder nearby. Dried mud caked his body from head to toe. With hands folded upon his lap, he stared straight ahead at nothing in particular. A stony frown blended into cracks of mud. His pouty attitude had replaced itself with a potent air of *so done with this.*

Phil had abandoned his obsessive petting of Ross for a careful examination of Gamon, his new favorite thing in the world. The hairy beast stood tall and strong, donning a thick leather vest with matching trousers. A heavy utility belt with numerous pouches completed the portrait of a buccaneering Bigfoot. With arms crossed and brow taut, he tolerated Phil's cheek pinches, horn pokes, and fur combing. Gamon batted away any curious attempts to do otherwise.

Ross and Steve watched from the ship's airlock, content to participate from afar.

Zoey turned to Gamon. "So you tracked this creep all the way from Durangoni?"

Gamon nodded. "Yup."

"But how?" Perra said. "Nobody has ever been able to track the Suth'ra. They're too smart for that."

"Well, the other one used a relay frequency to contact the Suth'ra station. My sniffers managed to uncover it. Maybe they cut some corners in order to arrange the hit, which is kind of sloppy if you ask me. But, it allowed me to create a targeted sniffer, which is how I found *him*."

Frank shifted his lips.

"Which means," Zoey said, tapping her chin, "that the entire collective is coming after Max, not just one."

Max lifted a sullen gaze to Gamon. "What do they want with me?"

Gamon shrugged. Phil slid a tentacle over his shoulder and hooked a vest pocket. Gamon smacked it away without batting an eye.

Perra narrowed her eyes and turned to Phil. "Wait a tick, you *knew* the Suth'ra were after Max."

Phil halted his incessant study of Gamon.

Perra pointed at Frank. "And you *knew* this bastard was on the planet."

Phil sprouted a pair of hands and knocked knuckles.

"So why in Tim's name didn't you warn us?"

Phil lowered his arms and sank a bit. "I like visitors," he said in a timid voice.

Zoey nabbed Perra's arm. "Phil is impartial, you know that. He has the social skills of a needy toddler."

Phil waved at Frank, who stiffened and looked away.

"Still," Perra said, yanking her arm back. "Even a blob like Phil should understand the concept of imminent danger. This thing captured Max and crawled away before anyone even noticed."

A restless silence fell upon the group, leaving them to the dull roar of the waterfall in the distance. Perra crossed her arms and stepped away, content to stew inside her own head. Zoey sighed and glanced at Gamon, who responded with a half-grin. A fresh tentacle crawled over his shoulder and walked its way down his chest. The beast plucked the invasive noodle and crushed it, drawing a yelp from Phil. He slurped it back into his bloated mass and whimpered like a scolded dog. Moments later, a new tentacle slithered over Gamon's shoulder. He closed his eyes and shook his head.

"So," Ross said from the airlock. "Just throwing this out there. We captured an active member of the Suth'ra Society, which I'm pretty sure is unprecedented. Ergo ... he would fetch a handsome sum on the black market. Just saying."

Perra responded with a stupefied gaze. "You want to *sell* him?"

"Nooo, no, no ..." Ross paused to read the room, then cocked an ear back. "Yes."

Perra tossed her arms into the air and cackled with irony, as if to call it quits on the entire plot. She sauntered over to Frank with hands at her waist. "So there you have it. The brainsack wants to fondle you and the cat wants to sell you into slavery. Would you like to know what's behind door number three?" Her unhinged demeanor sent chills down Frank's four spines.

"Sweetie," Zoey said. "Maybe we should—"

"Don't *sweetie* me," Perra said. "Are you not listening? This is dangerous territory, both morally and ethically. Are you seriously considering—"

"*Considering?*" Zoey took a firm step forward. "I'm not *considering* a goddamn thing. This fucker is a kidnapper out to murder your friend. *That* is worthy of consideration first and foremost."

Perra crossed her arms and hardened her gaze. "Do you not think I know that?"

"Well, *considering* your colorful outburst, I would hope you—"

"Stop!" Max said, sending a booming echo around the cavern. "Just, stop."

Perra bowed her head and looked away.

Zoey frowned and grasped her shoulder.

Max gathered his wits, lifted from the rock, and stomped over to Frank. He loomed over the creature with balled fists, panting with anger. "I haven't done anything to you! What the hell do you want from me?!"

All eight eyes focused on the Earthling.

Max spread his arms. "Well?"

Frank grinned. "Jerry, do you read?"

"Loud and clear, buddy."

"Now!"

A forked tongue shot from his mouth and wrapped itself around Max. He yanked the human to his lap as ribbons of light swirled around their bodies. With a blinding flash, they disappeared into nothingness.

CHAPTER 9

A wash of static crackled and faded, leaving the cave to the dull roar of the waterfall. Zoey, Perra, and Gamon gawked at the empty boulder Frank had sat upon moments earlier, their taut faces conveying multiple renditions of shock. Ross and Steve glanced at each other in a rare moment of mutual fluster. Phil continued his study of everything Gamon, as if nothing had happened.

"What the actual fuck?!" Zoey said, adding open arms for emphasis.

Everyone spun to Phil, who froze with the sudden influx of attention. He retracted all tentacles and cleared his throat (or whatever constituted a throat).

Perra whipped her eyes back and forth between Phil and the empty rock. "Where the hell did they go?"

Phil tilted a bit. "I figured that would be obvious."

Perra replied with a puckered expression that screamed *bite me, brainsack.*

Gamon returned to his slack-jawed study of the small boulder.

Ross leapt down from the airlock and trotted towards the group. "The Suth'ra have their prize. The only question now is, what—" Phil snatched Ross from the ground with a fresh tentacle and resumed his multi-handed petting. Ross grimaced and shook his head. "—what are we going to do about it?"

Zoey cupped her face with both hands and raked them through her choppy black hair. "The whole damn point of the Suth'ra Society is to remain hidden. These wackadoos go to extraordinary lengths to conceal their whereabouts. How can we track the untrackable?"

Gamon raised his hand. "Leave that to me."

* * *

Max awoke on a filthy sofa inside a discotheque filled with strobe lights, thumping music, and scantily clad aliens. It took him a moment to realize that this particular disco was, in fact, underwater. Or at the very least, the place was submerged in a pinkish liquid that Max could only assume was colored water. Panic set in for a split second, which his brain remedied after noticing it had unrestricted access to a pair of functioning gills. He glanced down at the rest of his body, still human, but all decked out in disco-era attire that made one question the wisdom of humanity. A flashy getup stretched from his feathered hair down to platform shoes. The entire ensemble looked as if a unicorn had puked on a velvet blanket.

Vibrant humanoids danced, mingled, and shouted over obnoxious music. Bright cocktails swished and swayed as if reacting to the familiar physics of air. A constant fizz of tiny bubbles lifted from every crack in the backlit floor. Max followed random orbs as they zigzagged up to the ceiling and disappeared. Drunken aliens in skimpy outfits danced upon elevated platforms with pulsing lights. They flailed to a synthesized beat supplied by a multi-headed DJ bobbing inside a cage of hologram turntables. One head pumped the crowd while another worked the console. The remaining six reveled in the chaos they created.

Max turned a waterlogged gaze to find a slender yellow creature standing beside the couch, resembling a stroked-out banana with crabby eyes.

"Oi!" the creature said at the top of its gills, causing Max to flinch. "Ew muss be that Earthly fella! A bally pleasure to meet ye!" It extended an arm stick with a brushy hand.

Max gripped the appendage, like squeezing a handful of dry spaghetti, only underwater. "He—hello."

The critter plopped onto the couch beside him, rippling the cushions and sending Max floating a few inches off the surface. "M'name Carl. N'you?"

"Max."

"Ye know, my sheila friend said there was an Earthman comin', but I dinna believe 'er. But slap me doodle and kick me quibbles, 'ere ye be!" His face stretched into a wide grin of gummy nubs, layered in rows like a toothless shark.

Max responded with a puzzled stare as he floated back down to the cushion. "Are you Australian?"

Carl laughed. "No Aussies here, mate." He leaned in and lowered his voice. "Unless you're into that sort of thing, then I 'ave a guy who knows a guy."

"No, um ..." Max scrunched his face. "*What?*"

"Ner'mind, mate, ner'mind." Carl glanced around the room in embarrassment.

Max's brain, having conceded rational thought from the first strobe light, decided enough was enough. "Okay, hold up. How is it even possible that I can hear you? This whole place is submerged underwater, yet I can hear you crisp and clear, like we're chilling on a park bench."

Carl chuckled and smacked Max on the back. "Oh mate, this ain' *water*. It's the liquefied membrane of—"

"Stop. Just, stop. I don't want to know."

Carl grinned and scooched closer. "Are ye swimmin' in tha roo tog yet?"

"The roo—*what?*"

Carl fished a green pill from his pocket and handed it to Max. "Oi, drop this 'ere on ye licker, count to ten, and thank me on the other side."

Max hesitated for a just-say-no second, then rolled his eyes, nabbed the pill, and placed it on his tongue. A nubby grin stretched across Carl's yellow face before melting into rainbows under an onslaught of psychedelic insanity. Hard lines morphed into wavy squiggles. Liquid evaporated into fluffy clouds. Thumping beats transformed into the smooth stylings of Barry Whitefish (rimshot). Max floated away into whatever groovy void would have him.

* * *

Max awoke on a dry sofa with his body upright, open palms to either side, feet flat on the floor, and head flopped on the rear cushion (standard frat house pass-out position). Lips smacked to moisten a parched tongue. The cool air, some of the cleanest he had ever tasted, came as a welcome reprieve. No gills or rave music, just a calm oxygen-rich environment. He opened his eyes to a dim pane of tarnished metal a few meters above the couch. Max decided to stare at the ceiling for a little while, a needed mental break before assessing the lunacy of the new predicament. An orb of soft light floated through his peripherals, detached and hovering just below the roof. A handful of orbs wandered the room like glowing soap bubbles. They bounced off walls and each other like a slow-motion pinball machine.

The creaks and clanks of whatever space he occupied needled a throbbing headache. Max lifted from the cushion and slumped forward, resting elbows on knees. Limp hands rubbed tired eyes and smoothed down a chaotic hairdo. He took time to admire the sofa, a tobacco leather chesterfield with high back and bronze rivets. Roaming eyes surveyed the room, a large metal box with no windows, a single door, and a slender yellow creature sitting in a folding chair. Max recoiled at the sight, then sighed with annoyance.

The creature stared at him with a composed demeanor. A set of eyestalks lifted from a domed head, rigid yet calm. Its fishy mouth frowned with an almost comical downturn, disposing of any intended menace. Slender arms and legs folded atop each other with the poise of a therapist about to dish out some uncomfortable truths.

"Greetings, Earthling," the creature said with a touch of arrogance.

"Hey, Carl."

The creature flinched and shifted his eyes. His rickety chair squeaked upon the floor as he struggled to regain a threatening presence.

Max glanced around the room again, then back to Carl. "Did you know that your smarty club is an *actual* club in another universe?"

Carl opened his mouth to respond, then clamped it shut in total bemusement.

Max clued into the fact that his body and clothes were clean. All mud had disappeared, leaving his skin nourished and garments fragrant. An armpit sniff, now minty fresh, left him with an uncomfortable sense of personal violation. He turned a miffed gaze to Carl. "Did you—ugh, do I even want to know?"

Carl shook his head.

Max fell back into the sofa and crossed his arms.

"Do you know where you are, Earthman?" Carl said, conjuring a ghoulish baritone.

"Somewhere on a Suth'ra station, I suppose."

Carl flinched and stammered, then recomposed himself. "The Suth'ra are a—"

"A bunch of super-smart alien nerds," Max said like a wiseass. "I know who you are, goober. The question is, what do you want from *me?*"

Carl huffed as if the human had insulted his wife. (Not that any members had spouses. Wanted? Sure. Had? Not a chance. Their legendary ineptitudes relegated courtship to the elusive realms of social competence.) Carl glared at an insolent Max before throwing in the towel. "Rutherford," he said with an uptick, as if to summon a snooty butler.

The door squeaked open, allowing a skinny robot to race inside. It stood a meter high with a large round head atop a brittle frame. The poor machine struggled with a top-heavy clumsiness, like a grapefruit stuck to a coat hanger. It slid to a stop and stiffened its gate. "Yes, Master Carl?"

"Please escort our guest to the Chamber of Fear."

Max lifted an eyebrow.

The robot's big red eye looked Max up and down, then turned back to Carl. "The subject is somewhat attractive, do you think it will work?"

"Of course it will work," Carl said. "No one can resist the Chamber's brain-melting torment. The Earthman needs a proper reduction before the Final Verdict."

"As you wish." The robot turned to Max and gestured to the door, the universal sign for *let's go, asshole.*

Max groaned as if commanded to take out the trash. He slapped the couch with both palms and climbed to his feet with a series of petulant gestures. Rutherford turned for the door with the human trudging behind. Carl smirked as he passed, prompting Max to lunge at him. The creature yipped with fright, jerked away, and tumbled out of his chair. Max chuckled like a pompous prick as Carl scrambled to regain some composure. For a split second, Max saw the appeal of bullying, then felt like a complete dick.

* * *

The tiny freighter crept through the waterfall and into a sunlit ravine. Hull thrusters rippled the river as the vessel climbed into the air and kicked towards the landing valley. Zoey and Perra studied the landscape with Ross in Perra's lap and Steve perched on Zoey's headrest. Gamon occupied most of the area behind the pilot seats, making one question how he managed to squeeze into the cockpit. They observed in restive silence, as if someone had cracked a tasteless joke without reading the room first. The vessel sailed over a steep hill, approaching the original landing site.

Gamon pointed to the valley edge. "He landed behind a large outcrop over there."

"Got it," Zoey said and steered the ship in said direction.

"There it is," Perra said, pointing off to the side.

"Good eye," Gamon said and patted her shoulder.

Just ahead, a round stealth ship poked out from behind a wall of jagged rock. Zoey slowed her approach and hovered the freighter a few meters off the ground, kicking up a cloud of dust and debris. She lowered the landing gear and floated to a rest, maintaining a comfortable distance. They stared at the floating black ball with a shared uncertainty.

"Are you sure this will work?" Perra said to Gamon.

"I don't see why not. Based on my own analysis, Suth'ra ships are primarily recon vessels, usually unmanned. Once their mission is complete, or in this case, their pilot teleports away, they return to the main station. At least, that's what I think happened with the other one."

"So why is it still here then?" Steve said.

"I intercepted the linkage signal after Frank left the ship. It still thinks he's here. In theory, the ship will return home once I drop the signal."

"With all of us inside," Perra said.

"Exactly."

Zoey sighed. "Alright, let's get to it then."

Nobody moved.

After a brief pause, Zoey turned and eyed Gamon.

"Oh, right, sorry," he said, then squirmed around the cockpit like a fat man in a phone booth.

Gamon squeezed through the narrow passageway and popped into the cargo bay like a cork from a bottle. Perra lowered Ross to the floor, halting a grooming session. She and Zoey lifted from their seats and slipped through the corridor with Ross and Steve trotting behind. Once inside the cargo bay, Ross resumed his disinterested licking while Steve pecked at a strand of frayed netting. Zoey opened a wall locker and nabbed a pair of plasma pistols. She tossed one to Perra and latched the other to her belt.

A dull rumble infected the air and shook the vessel as it approached. It thundered to a stop and proceeded to bang on the external airlock.

"Out in a minute," Perra said to Phil outside.

"Can I have the kitty?" Phil said in a muffled tone.

Zoey slapped a wall panel, opening the airlock.

Ross cocked his ears back. "Oh, you bit—"

Phil shot out a tentacle and plucked Ross from the ship.

Steve clucked at the disturbance, then resumed his pecks of random objects.

"You need a hand cannon?" Zoey said to Gamon.

"Nah, not going with."

"What? Why?"

"Do you see the size of that ship? It'll be cramped with you four, let alone with a big hairy beast like me."

Perra frowned and hugged his meaty arm.

"I'm sure you two will be fine. I dare say The Omen on a Suth'ra station will be chaotic enough without me getting in the way."

Zoey smirked and joined the group hug.

Steve flapped up to Gamon's noggin, clucked in a circle, then pecked at his nubby horns.

"Aaaany time now," Ross said from outside the ship.

"Itty bitty kitty," Phil said with Ross pressed against his flesh. A dozen hands stroked his fur in a knowing fashion. "Is a good kitty. My kitty. Phil's kitty."

Perra gave Gamon one final squeeze and broke from the embrace. She grabbed a sling bag from a nearby locker and turned for the airlock. "Okay, Philly, that's enough. Let the kitty go, we have to leave."

"Aw," Phil said and slumped like a pouty toddler.

Ross scurried out of his limp grasp and sprinted for the stealth ship. The group exited the freighter one by one with Steve bringing up the rear. He flapped to the ground and waddled towards the vessel. Phil snickered and reached for the snoodlecock.

Perra slapped the tentacle away. "No, you're done. You have had quite enough interaction this trip. Should last you a while, no?"

Phil sighed and softened to a whimper. "I guess."

Perra patted his leathery hide. "It was great to see you, though.

Thank you for the help and wish us luck."

Phil perked up a bit. "One more huggy hug?"

Perra turned to Zoey and grinned.

Zoey rolled her eyes. "Sure."

Phil squeed and clapped a pair of tentacles. He sprouted a dozen more and wrapped them around the Mulgawats. A wandering noodle crept over to Gamon, pinched his cheek, and slithered around his waist.

Gamon narrowed his eyes. "Don't even think ab—"

Phil yanked them all into his bloated mass. He twisted and turned with his interpretation of a goodbye hug, then spat them onto the ground with fresh sheens of mucus. The blob trembled and sank into a pool of contentment.

Zoey wiped her face and flung slime from her fingertips. She grimaced and turned an annoyed gaze to Perra. "Was it worth it?"

Perra smirked. "Philly has always been a good friend to us. A little love goo isn't going to hurt you."

Gamon groaned with disgust while climbing to his feet. Slime dripped from a drenched mane, flattening his springy curls. Raising his arms, he recoiled at the sight of clumpy fur hanging like sheets of damp moss. He opened his mouth to voice repulsion, but his stammering brain failed to conjure the appropriate words. Arms flopped to his side, squeezing globs of mucus down his legs. He traded disgust for irk and tossed a glare at Perra.

She responded with a doe-eyed smile. "Sorry, Gammy."

Gamon sighed and squished towards the ship.

Zoey snickered as she lifted from the dirt. "He is never going to forget that."

"Yeah, probably." Perra grabbed Zoey's hand, sprung to her feet, and turned to a puddled Phil. "You mind watching the ship while we're away?"

"Aye aye," Phil said, adding a limp salute.

"Thanks buddy."

The pair turned for the stealth ship and pressed forward, leaving gooey tracks with each step. Zoey slung mucus from her pistol while

Perra wiped her sling bag. They wrung their hair and clothes along the way.

Zoey sighed. "This should be an interesting adventure."

"Max is family. He would do the same for us."

"Not saying he wouldn't. I'm just worried."

"How so?"

"Hollow Hold may have been a mysterious hellhole, but at least there were bits of information to gather. Nobody in the 'verse has ever seen a Suth'ra station, let alone been to one. We're going into this completely blind."

"We've been through worse, no?"

Zoey snorted. "We're about to crash a wandering trash heap full of super-geniuses. I'm fairly certain that we have no comparable."

"Point taken."

The stealth ship floated a foot above the ground, locked in place by a magnetic anchor. Its smooth hull resembled an unblemished wrecking ball, primed for destruction or a pop diva music video. Gamon poked his way around the vessel, gathering as much insight as he could. He input some nav data into his comdev, compiled a command sequence, and initiated launch prep. The orb responded with a clank and hiss, drawing a grunt of success. The top half unlatched and floated upwards, spilling puffs of steam like an old school locomotive. Ross and Steve fought for shotgun, eager to rid themselves of Phil and his creepy planet.

"You ladies ready?" Gamon said.

Perra sighed. "As ready as we'll ever be."

She hoisted herself into the capsule and paused to study the interior. The tiny cockpit sat dormant, as if abandoned years ago. Perra slid her hand across the lifeless console, a narrow plane of murky glass. The flimsy pilot seat teetered as an afterthought, like an office chair bolted to the frame. Not much else greeted the eye, just an empty shell fit for hauling whatever got tossed inside it.

Zoey crossed her arms and turned to Gamon. "So what can we expect from this thing?"

Gamon shrugged. "Not a clue, to be honest. Just hold on tight and hope for the best."

"That's reassuring."

"If it were anyone else, I'd be worried." Gamon grinned and extended a paw.

Zoey returned the grin and grabbed his fuzzy mitt. After a firm shake, she grasped the edge and yanked herself into the ship.

"Good hunting. I hope you find your friend."

"Thank you, Gammy," Perra said.

Steve clucked as he searched for a cozy pocket of space to occupy. Ross did the same and groused with every turn. Perra lowered to her knees behind the pilot seat, allowing Zoey to step over and plop into the chair. The group poked and shoved each other, as if learning to fly a bathtub. Zoey tucked her shoulders and tossed Gamon a thumbs-up. He nodded and tapped his comdev. The top half floated down with a magnetic hum and sealed them inside. A sharp clank and latch left them cramped together in complete darkness. Zoey knocked the wall and flicked the console, breaking a needling silence.

"Now what?" Ross said.

"Hell if I know," Zoey said.

Steve cleared his throat. "I should probably mention that I am severely claustrophobic. We have about eight seconds before I lose control of my faculties."

"I know a funny joke," Ross said. "What came first? The snoodlecock or the broken neck it suffered after freaking out in a broom closet?"

A nervy silence responded.

"The punch line needs work," Steve said.

"Dibs on the drumsticks," Zoey said.

The vessel burst into life, flooding the interior with deep red hues. Blips, pings, and hums filled the tiny space. Alien characters sped across the console as the ship prepped for departure. The viewport flashed and faded, opening a thin gander. The sliver expanded around the group and washed over the interior like a giant sunroof, unveiling a sweeping vista while retaining an opaque hull. The group twisted their gazes around the enclosure, taking their final looks

97

around the pristine landscape.

Gamon backed away with comdev in hand, studying the launch readings while keeping a safe distance. The vessel released its magnetic grip and floated upwards in complete silence. Gamon eyed the sphere in wonder as it gained a jolt of momentum, sailed into the atmosphere, and disappeared into a sliver of purple light.

"Wow," he said, still staring into the sky.

A pair of tentacles reached up from behind and pinched his cheeks. Gamon groaned and shook his head.

CHAPTER 10

Max followed Rutherford through a never-ending maze of pod components. A narrow service tunnel brought them to the hatch of a cramped landing module. The ladder inside crawled through the ventilation shaft of a transport shuttle, which docked to an old spy satellite full of dangling wires, and so on and so forth. Navigating the tangled mess of a Suth'ra station meant crawling, ducking, climbing, tripping, squeezing, and more crawling. The wonky gravity needled the senses, like trying to navigate an M. C. Escher painting. Once inside a normal room, one gained an appreciation of stretching space.

Rutherford stepped along the inverted wall of a cargo pod and dropped through a sideways airlock into a spacious corridor. Max followed with arms outstretched, opting for a more cautious approach. He palmed the door and dangled from the airlock before releasing his grip. His legs hit the floor at an awkward angle, bending his momentum into the nearest wall. He thumped the unforgiving metal with a stiff shoulder, drawing a grunt of discomfort. A brief pause with mumbled curses allowed his brain enough time to reorient baffled muscles. His eyes wandered the passage, a haunting place full of grimy grates and crawling steam, creating the ideal ambience for an alien horror movie.

The robot stood in the center of the corridor with arms crossed. A tapping metal foot lifted sharp clinks into the air. His narrowing red eye conveyed a waning patience.

"I'm coming, jeez, keep your pants on," Max said.

Rutherford glanced down at his skinny legs, then around the immediate area, back to Max, then back to his legs.

Max rolled his eyes. "It's just a saying. What, you don't have idioms here?" He lifted his weary body from the wall and slogged towards the robot.

Rutherford grumbled, about-faced, and continued down the corridor. He turned a corner and stopped in front of a large airlock. The door panel seemed wider and heavier than most, like the entrance to a holding cell. Rutherford stared at it in silence, as if contemplating whether or not he went to the right place. Moments later, the wall panel pinged and glowed with a crimson hue. The door unlatched with a loud thunk, releasing a hiss of pressurized air. It slid open with the sluggish pace of a battle arena revealing the final boss.

A thin cloud of steam dissipated to reveal a large empty room, about the size of a fast-food restaurant. The chamber radiated sterility with every surface devoid of feature. No fixtures, no panel lines, just a vacuum-like state with every corner rounded to create a seamless void. In the center, a small table and a pair of chairs affixed themselves to the floor. Their drab coloring matched the room, as if sprouted like furniture-shaped flowers.

Rutherford glanced at Max, then stepped into the room. Max followed him through the door with a peculiar sense of placid fascination. He glanced over to a side wall where a towering one-way mirror filled the space, itself a featureless plane that blended into the wall it occupied. He caught his own reflection and squinted.

"What the—" Max trotted over to the mirror to discover an array of unfamiliar features. He looked like himself, only with defined lines, a chiseled jaw, and dreamy blue eyes. To put it another way, he was hot, at least by Earth standards. "Holy hell, *that* is the tweak?" He opened his come-hither lips to reveal perfect teeth. Twisting his head back and forth painted the shadows of prominent cheekbones.

He raised a dimpled chin and poked at a manly Adam's apple. "I mean, I'm not complaining by any stretch, but this would have been very nice to have *back home.*" He grinned, winked, and click-pointed at his reflection. His complete lack of concern bubbled from a cartoonish level of self-confidence.

Rutherford, now standing beside the table, expelled the robotic equivalent of an impatient cough. Max stepped away from his enchanting image, adding a playful smirk before spinning towards the table. He stopped, turned back to his reflection, chuckled like an idiot, added a cocky flex, then turned back to the robot. After a few more steps, he spun around again and decided to shuffle backwards in order to admire his handsome image. The robot shook its head as the human approached. With a final strut and twirl, Max added the pompous lean and lazy stare of a suburban cowboy.

Rutherford pointed to the nearest chair. "Sit."

Max plopped into the seat and kicked back with hands hooked in his pockets, channeling every arrogant prick who had ever pricked. He turned back to his distant reflection, again, and up-nodded.

"Wait here," the robot said.

Max opened his palms and smirked, the universal jock mime for *whatever, dude.*

Rutherford tossed an irked glare at the one-way mirror, then turned and exited the room. The airlock door rumbled shut, leaving Max to an eerie silence. He glanced around the enclosure while humming a nonsense melody just to break the dead air. Bored fingers rapped upon the table surface.

Behind the mirror, Fio stared at Max with arms crossed and brow furrowed. A wormy humanoid manned a console nearby, prepping the Chamber of Fear for action. A white lab coat clung to his grubby body like a cape. The garment clearly wished to adorn another species, or at the very least, anything with shoulders. The boneless scientist adjusted his thick glasses, tweaked some final commands, then offered a *good-to-go* thumbs-up. Fio smirked and returned his gaze to the antsy human drumming on the chamber table.

A side door slid open, allowing Rutherford to clank into the control room. He settled beside Fio and crossed his arms in echoed disgust. "This isn't going to work, you know."

"Of course it will," Fio said with a dismissive tone. "No one can resist the Chamber's brain-melting torment."

"Carl said the same thing. Like, the *exact* same thing. You guys must have flashcards or something."

Fio tossed a stink eye to the insolent robot, then nodded to the controller. The wormy creature nodded back, reached beside the console, and grabbed a small bag of popcorn. A pudgy tentacle stretched across the console and tapped a large green icon. He settled back in his chair and munched away as the chamber dimmed.

Max maintained his too-cool-to-care demeanor, unfazed by the sudden veil of darkness. A dull hum filled the room as hologram images started to piece together all around him. The photo-real depictions created the eloquent atmosphere of a posh restaurant, complete with dainty waiters, racks of wine, and sleek lanterns hanging from the ceiling. Muffled conversations imbued the space, interweaving with classical music and the delicate clinks of glasses. The table filled itself with hors d'oeuvres, crusty bread, and an array of cutlery. Max watched the scene unfold in wide-eyed disbelief. He plucked a napkin from the table and examined it. The cloth hung from his grip with actual weight. He rolled the fabric between his fingers and could sense the texture. A complete sensory immersion with gravity, density, and consequence.

As a final touch, the chamber added an attractive woman in a silky black dress to the seat across the table. She flirted a bit, then launched into a poignant discussion about politics and her mother.

Fio grinned. "I give him five minutes."

The worm creature grunted. "Three, tops."

Rutherford shook his head. "You're both idiots."

* * *

A flash of purple light spat the stealth ship into open space. Zoey, Perra, Ross, and Steve glanced around a vast ocean of nothing.

No galaxies, nebulas, or asteroids, just an infinite backdrop of distant stars. The vessel floated in the empty black, infecting everyone with a profound sense of detachment. The console chirped as it established contact with the Suth'ra station somewhere nearby. A linkage icon pinged and turned red, silencing the cabin. The ship tilted downwards and kicked towards a bright star. Tick after tick, the star expanded. It grew into a reflective snowflake, then morphed into the crude outline of a space station. Soon after, the colossal trash heap revealed itself, dropping three jaws and a beak.

The patchwork vessel resembled a derelict space station that never treated a benign yet aggressive tumor. The tumor, realizing that its host had no interest in treating it, expanded to a point where the host became superfluous. (As a simple illustration, imagine thousands of trucks, trailers, forklifts, mainframe computers, plasma televisions, farm equipment, and discarded pieces of sheet metal plugged into a handful of oil rigs. That might provide a sense of what this horrid monstrosity looked like. Odd would be an understatement. This thing was downright gnarly.)

Steve clucked with pure bewilderment, slow enough to actually vocalize the word *buck*.

"My stars," Perra said, equally shocked.

Zoey shook her head. "How in the 'verse does that thing even function?"

"It doesn't, which is kind of the point," Ross said. "It's just a roamer. As long as they can recycle food and air, the rest is immaterial."

The franken-station pulled the stealth ship towards its mangled body. The group ogled in silence as the metal beast consumed the space around them. The tiny vessel slipped through a crevasse and snaked its way through a maze of twisted components. It emerged into an expansive corridor lined with blinking piles of electronic debris, resembling a nightmarish nursery used to birth murder bots. At the rear of the creepy hollow, a towering wall of round ports loomed as a destination. Floodlights around the perimeter bathed it with a golden sheen, giving it the unsettling appearance of a giant wasp eye.

The stealth vessel floated towards an empty dock and slipped through a transparent green barrier that served as an airlock. Once inside, it lowered to the ground and locked into place with a magnetic grip.

The top half unlatched, twisted free, and floated away, gifting them a blast of clean air (as well as a much-needed stretch). Zoey and Perra traded nods of success, but a poofed Ross turned their attention to a large service droid racing towards them. Its wide base, bony frame, and spidery head gave it the appearance of a steampunk sunflower.

"Shit!" Ross said, then scampered out of the vehicle.

Steve flapped away as Zoey and Perra spilled over the side and followed Ross behind a nearby stack of crates. The robot paused to survey the ruckus, then realized it didn't care in the slightest. It plunged its gadget-laden head into the lower half of the vessel and got to work. Steve landed atop the crates and hopped down to the floor. After a quick regroup, they peered around the stack.

An extensive service area unfolded before their eyes, backlit with a sterile green light. A dozen droids poked and prodded around the room. Welding sparks arched through the air and bounced on a smooth floor marked with maglev tracks. The mellow hum of magnetic propulsion blanketed the space as robots darted from task to task. Countless cords dangled from the ceiling like moss hanging from branches. Massive claws swayed from mounted tracks, resembling an old arcade game ready to fish for prizes.

"So what now?" Perra said.

Zoey shook her head. "For once, I have no idea."

"We should scout a bit," Ross said. "Get a layout of the interior, maybe stumble upon some intel."

Zoey turned a skeptical gaze to the feline. "So what, we just wander around?"

"Yes, actually. This is a Suth'ra station. Nobody is going to think twice about you being here. For all they know, you solved a riddle and joined like everyone else. And besides, it's not like anyone will look you in the eye and say hello. Just act like you belong and everything will be fine."

Perra shrugged. "I guess that makes sense."

"Also bear in mind, these eggheads developed the most sophisticated cloaking tech in the entire universe, and regard it as such. We can already see that security is nonexistent, probably because they dismiss the possibility of infiltration. They would sooner normalize our presence than admit their tech is flawed. Hell, I bet the droids aren't even programmed to second guess an unfamiliar face."

Steve clucked and trotted out into the open room.

"Steve!" Zoey said with a harsh whisper. "What the hell are you—"

"Bacock!" he said at the top of his tiny lungs.

A dozen service droids stopped and turned towards the colorful snoodlecock standing alone beside a stack of crates. Silence infected the room. Zoey, Perra, and Ross gawked at the bird through horrified faces. Steve flapped a fresh round of feathers into the air. The droids studied the creature for a moment, traded puzzled glances, then resumed their tasks at hand. The hum of automation refilled the room. The group exhaled a collective sigh as Steve waddled back behind the crates.

"That was lucky," Ross said. "I pulled that last part out of my ass."

Perra thumped her back against the crates and covered her racing heart.

"Pull that shit again," Zoey said to Ross, "and I'll dump you on Phil's Place as a permanent squeeze toy."

Ross puckered his jowls and shook off an involuntary shiver.

A series of sharp clanks snagged the group's attention. They turned to find Steve pecking at an air vent along the wall. He jerked his gaze back to the group.

"You two scout. In the meantime, the feline and I will conduct some stealthy recon."

"No, we shouldn't split up," Zoey said.

"You ladies can blend," Ross said. "But a house cat and a snoodlecock wandering about may raise a few eyebrows. Or at the very least, grumble some stomachs."

Zoey groused, then nodded in agreement.

"Let's see what we can find and meet back here in 20 marks."

"Better yet, establish a comlink with us." Perra reached into her satchel and retrieved a pair of neural-link earbuds, a type of radio wave transmitter that interacted with the user's neural pathways. The devices transmitted motioned words as clear dialogue. She enabled them with a click and flick, causing them to glow atop her hand. Zoey plucked one and tucked it into her ear. Perra did the same.

"You copy?" Perra mouthed.

"Loud and clear," Zoey mouthed back.

"All linked up," Ross said, transmitting his voice.

Steve jerked his head back and forth in confusion.

"I'm a cyborg," Ross said to Steve.

Steve paused for thought, then nodded. "Oooh ... that explains a lot."

Perra fished a multi-tool from her satchel and knelt in front of the air vent. She detached the panel, set it aside, and turned to Ross. "Keep us updated. We'll do the same. Mind your step and stay out of sight. We may not be in a position to help should things go south."

"Understood."

Steve clucked and tilted his head.

Ross trotted into the vent. "Follow me, KFC."

Steve stood where he was, trading glances between the vent and the Mulgawats.

A sigh echoed from the vent. "C'mon, doofus!"

The snoodlecock clucked, hopped, and clanked into the vent. Perra reattached the cover and lifted to her feet. Zoey scanned the room and pointed to a far corner where a pair of service doors swung behind an emerging droid.

"How about there?"

"Works for me."

Zoey took a deep breath and stepped out from behind the crate stack, exposing herself to the bustling bay. Perra adjusted her sling pack and followed. The droids paid them no mind as they crept across the room and slipped through the swinging doors.

* * *

Back in the Chamber of Fear, Max chatted up a gorgeous blonde in a silky black dress. A posh waiter named Francois (Max knew this because he asked) swung by the table from time to time to top off the wine glass dangling between his fingers. Max grew to appreciate the sweet, subtle nuances of Haffonico blends from the Xon Kyne province (also because he asked). He laughed, smiled, and played the scene like a well-tuned fiddle.

Fio leaned on the one-way mirror with palms pressed to the glass and eyes locked onto the human. Jerry and Frank stood behind him in contrasting states of shock. All eight of Frank's eyes refused to blink for fear of missing a single tick. Jerry's face twisted its way through horror and fascination. Karmo continued to munch on his popcorn, albeit at a slow and captivated pace. Rutherford shook his head as Max's cocky voice filled the room with flirty banter.

"Dude got game," Karmo said.

Jerry huffed and flailed. "What kind of sorcery is this?! The dude is blathering about pizza and pancakes. I mean, I get it, they're delicious, but this dialogue has zero substance. She should have tuned out long ago."

"How long have they been going?" Frank said.

"Almost a full c-mark," Karmo said.

The group gasped.

Fio wheezed with resentment. "The woman is actually *listening* to him! He's talking out his ass and she's hanging onto every word. What the hell, Karmo? Did you actually program her like that?"

Karmo studied the scene with fierce curiosity. "I, uh ... never planned for this. It was out of the realm of testable possibilities."

"This is what I was trying to tell you," Rutherford said. "The Earthman is attractive. He's a pretty boy on his planet. It doesn't matter *what* he says because he says it with undue confidence. Earth females are capable of overlooking a *lot* of bullshit when a dude looks and talks like that."

Jerry leaned over to Karmo. "You're taping this, right? It could be a breakthrough in carnal science."

"Oh yes," Karmo said while crunching.

"Cap the allure scale," Fio said to Karmo.

Karmo flinched popcorn onto the console. "*What?* That has never been done before. It could fry his brain."

"I don't care! The Earthman needs to suffer!"

Karmo sighed and removed his glasses. He set his snack aside and tapped the console. A scale appeared on the screen with the dial set at 30%. He dangled a shaking tentacle over the control. "Are you sure you want to do this? Be aware, we are entering uncharted territory."

Jerry and Frank traded worried glances.

Fio narrowed his eyes. "Do it."

Karmo took a deep breath and swiped the scale to 100%. The woman exploded into a million pixels, filling the room with a shimmering snow. Max jerked to his feet and ogled the twinkling cloud. Hologram ribbons swirled around the chamber with the grace of a ballerina. They returned to the opposite chair and began to reassemble. Legs appeared, then a waist, chest, neck, all building up to the completed image of Angelina Jolie.

"Hello, Max," she said, taking a seductive sip of wine.

Max froze with utter stupefaction.

A cautious silence infected the control room.

Frank fainted.

Max thought for a tick, smirked, then sauntered back to his seat. "Well well well, how *you* doin'?"

Angelina replied with a playful smile.

"Fuck me sideways," Fio said in disbelief. "He thinks he has a chance."

Rutherford sighed. "Like I said, he's a young stud with a big hairy ego. The world is handed to him on a silver platter. He gets rewarded for doing absolutely nothing. You're not seeing things. He *actually* thinks he's going to hit that."

Jerry plopped into a chair and sulked. "I worked hard for my physics degree."

"And you're a better person for it," Karmo said, patting his shoulder.

Jerry whimpered and fidgeted with a shirt button.

"Kill the simulation," Fio said.

Karmo tapped a large red icon. The scene flickered and faded, leaving Max to a darkened room. House lights kicked on and the chamber reset. Max slammed a fist onto the table and turned to the one-way mirror.

"Not cool! I had her on the hook!"

CHAPTER 11

Zoey and Perra weaved their way through a labyrinth of old utility shuttles. A half-closed airlock led into a grimy service tunnel. An emergency exit linked to a crew entrance. They squeezed through the window of an abandoned loader and into a bunker filled with hanging laundry. Dirty sheets and three-legged pants swayed from floating hooks attached to nothing. They ducked around the garments, slipped through a wall portal, and emerged inside a spacious corridor with lighting strips and grated floors. Touch panels glowed with idle hues, marking hatch points to parts unknown. To the left, the tunnel disappeared into a distant rise. To the right, a nearby junction split it in two.

Perra glanced back and forth. "Which way do you want to go?"

Zoey shrugged. "I haven't the foggiest idea."

A nearby panel pinged green, hooking their attention. The hatch below it clanked and creaked open with a shrill whine, allowing a spidery alien to squeeze into the tunnel. A plump and hairless body rested on seven legs and a stump. It adjusted to the wonky gravity and turned towards the Mulgawats. A pair of stunted arms grasped a thick manual and a comically large protractor. Three black eyes studied the book as the creature moseyed down the corridor. Zoey hardened her stance and palmed her plasma pistol. Perra took a step back and plotted their escape. The alien tossed them a glance as it passed, using peripherals to eschew eye contact. It harbored zero interest and proceeded down the passage with eyes affixed to the book.

Zoey relaxed her gate and straightened her jacket with a shoulder roll. "Huh, I guess Ross was right."

Perra studied a jagged ceiling full of random panels and ducts. Her eyes crawled down an adjacent wall to a dangling latch. She unhooked it and opened a small cubby. Inside, a hairless rodent pedaled atop a tiny exercise bike. It stared straight ahead and kept pedaling, as if oblivious to the giant orange humanoid staring at it. Without a word, Perra shut the door and rejoined Zoey, content to forget the visual.

"Such a weird place."

"An enormous understatement."

"It feels like we're at a carnival, only nobody is having fun." Perra paused for thought. "Actually, it's exactly like a carnival."

Zoey glanced back and forth, then nodded towards the junction. "Let's go that way."

They hiked down the tunnel and veered to the right, for no compelling reason whatsoever. The passage twisted and turned like a corn maze before ending at a flickering room full of busted monitors. They ducked around sparking wires and pushed through a drapery of plastic into an adjacent room. Spectrum lamps hung from the ceiling, feeding rows of fruit-bearing plants. Automated droids hovered around the enclosure, tending to the crops. Zoey carved through a thick mist with Perra in tow. At the other end, they opened an old crank hatch and slipped inside. A blast of chilled air filled their lungs as a psychedelic mural unfolded. Widened eyes scanned a vast hollow full of iridescent sculptures. A shadowy tree adorned the center, torn from the pages of a creepy children's book. Twisted branches stabbed through a macabre tree house, creating the physical manifestation of a hallucinogenic nightmare.

"Now that's downright unsettling," Perra said.

Zoey sighed. "This is getting us nowhere."

"We need a better plan."

"I may have one," Ross said over the comlink.

*   *   *

Back at the Chamber of Fear, a fog of defeat infected the control room. Fio glared at his captive human through the one-way mirror. With brow taut and hands at his waist, he conveyed the same contempt as a wearied boss wondering how to handle a problem employee. Max stood on the other side, studying his reflection with a cheesy grin. He rolled up his sleeves and flexed, admitting everyone behind the mirror to the gun show. They all groaned and rolled their eyes.

"So what now?" Karmo said from the console.

Fio maintained his spiteful stare and lowered his voice to a grumble. "The Earthling has bested the Chamber of Fear, an unfortunate setback. However, I sincerely doubt that his tenacity can withstand ..." He paused for effect and returned to a high-pitched squeal. "The Arena of Suffering!"

Karmo gasped.

Frank fainted, again.

"Sweet Sagan," Jerry said. "That would likely kill him before he reaches the Final Verdict."

Fio smirked and narrowed his gaze. "No. We will have trained emergency medical personnel on-site should things get hairy."

"Trained emergency med—" Jerry huffed and shook his head. "Jeez, just say *Corina*. What is it with you and your political word salads?"

Fio clenched his lips, then swallowed the retort. "Fine. We'll make sure *Corina* is there."

"Thank you. Was that so hard?"

Fio ignored him and turned to Rutherford. "Escort the prisoner to the Arena of Suffering. Wait for us there while I summon the spectators."

"Aye aye," the robot said and clanked away.

* * *

Zoey and Perra slid down a frayed rope into a storage bunker. Zoey hit the floor first and hopped aside to survey the space. Perra hit behind her and eyed the hole above to assure their privacy. They glanced around a mid-sized room full of crates, barrels, and other containers. The dim lighting and dank air created the vibe of a spooky basement.

"Now where?" Zoey said.

"There's a door panel to your right," Ross said through the comlink. "Opens outward, just push."

Zoey stepped over to the wall and studied the smooth surface. She ran a finger through the grime and uncovered a panel line. Pressing both hands to the wall, she gave it a stiff push. The panel squeaked open, revealing a bright hallway. She took a cautious step into the passage and glanced down each side. Rows of gaudy wall sconces threw cones of light onto the ceiling. Plush carpeting lined the floor from end to end. The radiant amber walls featured numerous pieces of abstract art housed in anti-geometric frames. Zoey gawked at the space with a slow spin, as if yanked into a surrealist fantasy. Perra stepped inside, closed the door behind her, and mirrored Zoey's dangling chin.

"This place keeps getting weirder and weirder," Perra said.

"Left corridor, third door on your right," Ross said.

"How do you know all this?" Zoey said.

"I'll explain when you get here."

They trotted past one door and hugged a bend before stopping dead in their tracks. A giant slug crawled towards them with sunken eyes, plump lips, and spiky protrusions. Its striped body took up most of the hallway. The creature inched closer and closer, leaving a trail of glowing slime in its wake. A skinny tentacle clutched a tablet device while another tapped furiously across the surface, like a young teenager venting melodramatic grievances to social media. Zoey and Perra pressed their backs against the wall as the slug slid by on a plane of mucus. It squished and belched as it passed, paying no mind to the orange visitors. A pungent aroma assaulted the air.

Perra cringed. "What the—ugh."

Zoey covered her mouth and nose. "Smells like boiled vomit."

"Keep going," Ross said. "You're almost there, just two doors down on the right."

Zoey and Perra lifted from the wall and tromped down the hallway, careful to avoid the sheen of slime on the floor. Zoey covered her nose with her shirt while Perra fanned her face with both hands. Arriving at the door, they burst inside, slammed it shut, and drew several breaths of clean air. They glanced around a tiny kitchenette with a sink counter and wall cabinets, offering the cramp coziness of their familiar freighter. A breakfast table rested against the wall with two flimsy chairs. Perra plopped her bag onto the table and took a much-needed seat.

"We're here," Zoey said.

"Excellent," Ross said. "Incoming."

A ceiling tile slid away above the cabinet. Steve hopped down, clucked a hello, and flapped to the countertop. Ross plunked onto the cabinet, then glanced back to the opening and nodded. A small cleanbot hovered through the hole and glided down to the counter, its large red eye surveying the room as it descended. Ross resealed the hole, then bounded to the floor and leapt into the other chair.

"Hello, ladies," he said. "Glad you could make it."

Steve jerked his head from side to side.

The spidery robot lifted a tiny hand and saluted.

"What the hell is that?" Zoey said.

"It's a Hygienics Droid. They call 'em cleanbots, which is kind of tyrannical if you ask me. I call it Hy-D and she's our key to finding Max."

"A cleaning droid?" Perra said with a skeptical tone.

"Yup, but not just any droid. As you know, the Suth'ra are a finicky bunch with a low tolerance for chitchat. They just want everything to do their jobs without being told. Thus, in a remarkable stroke of social avoidance, they equipped all of their service droids with artificial intelligence. And if you are a sentient robot tasked with cleaning up after ungrateful slobs, how long would it take you to throw in the towel? No pun intended."

"Erp op dik dee neg," Hy-D said.

"What did she say?" Perra said.

Ross cleared his throat. "I believe the phrase was, 'fuck those hookers.'"

Steve cluck-chuckled.

"So you can understand her?" Zoey said.

"Yeah, just a common form of droid-speak. Think of it like Luke and R2-D2. They can understand each other, but refuse to speak the same language for whatever dumbass reason. Course, the whole dynamic is a farce because C-3PO caters his speech like a goddamn gentleman."

Steve tilted his head. "Why would you create a loop of translation using two different lexicons on opposing ends of a conversation? That makes no sense."

"Irka pek dap heek dur," Hy-D said.

Ross snorted. "She said—"

"I got it, thanks." Steve glared at the bot. "And you can kiss my cloaca, she-droid."

Hy-D balled her tiny fists and shook them at Steve, who growled in response.

"That's enough." Zoey sighed and shuffled over to the counter. She crossed her arms, leaned back, and turned her attention to Ross. "So we have a disgruntled droid, which is all fine and dandy, but how does that help us?"

Ross raised an eyebrow. "Is it not obvious?"

Zoey sneered and rolled a hand, signaling to get on with it.

"This is a Hygienics Droid tasked with cleaning a Suth'ra station, an unmappable maze of insanity. Ergo ..."

"She knows the entire station," Perra said.

Ross nodded. "Exactly. That's how we guided you here. Not only that, but the droids overhear everything. Hy-D was present at the council meeting that debated Max's fate."

Zoey stiffened as Perra leapt to her feet.

"Where is he now?"

"Abo eek drit carbi oka."

Ross cocked his ears. "They're taking him to the Arena of Suffering."

Steve gasped, then pecked at a few crusties in the sink.

Perra covered her mouth.

Zoey turned a worried gaze to the droid. "What do they do there?"

"Cark ip dwan sweta."

"Unspeakable atrocities," Ross said.

"Gep curk dreg—" The droid sighed, then spun through a quick reset. "There, how's that?" The metallic yet amiable female voice caught everyone by surprise.

Zoey glared at the droid. "That would have been helpful from the start."

The droid glared back, took to the air, and hovered up to eye-level. "Listen, Orangina. I don't know you, I don't like you, and I sure as hell ain't helping you for the lolz." Hy-D extended a tiny finger and pointed it at Zoey's eyeball mere inches away. "You're in *my* house. And if you don't like it, you best know that I can fit into all sorts of uncomfortable cavities."

Steve winced.

"Ooookay then," Ross said, trying to defuse the tension. "Let's not forget that we're all on the same team here and that Max is the primary focus."

Zoey buried visual daggers into the droid. She snatched it out of the air with a swift hand, drawing a yelp. "*You* best know that *we* are not the Suth'ra, and anything you crawl into may feel good enough to keep you there."

The robot recoiled and pooped a spark.

Zoey released her grip, allowing Hy-D to resume flight. The droid floated over to the table, landed with a stumble, and shivered. Perra hooked her satchel and tossed it over a shoulder.

"Can we drop the dick fight and focus on Max? He's in trouble and needs our help."

"Agreed," Zoey said.

"Second," Ross said.

"Porkins," Steve said.

The group turned confused gazes to the snoodlecock in the sink.

"Oh, my apologies. That's Yarnwal for *hell yeah!*" Steve accented with a wingspread, shedding a few feathers.

"Anyway," Perra said, regaining the floor. "Hy-D, can you map us a path to the Arena of Suffering?"

"Sure can." The robot projected a hologram rendition of the complex. A blinking dot denoted their current position, which morphed into a red line that weaved its way to the opposite end of the station. The countless twists and turns resembled a baffled snake suffering an epileptic seizure. An army of blue dots, denoting life forms, descended upon the target. "Given the average run speed of a healthy Mulgawat, I estimate that it would take you four c-marks to get there, assuming you don't stop for snacks or bathroom breaks."

"They're already assembling," Perra said. "We'll never make it in time."

Steve twisted his head with sudden interest and flapped over to the table beside the hologram. He whipped his beak across the station, spinning it for a better view. A few pecks zoomed into their immediate area. Another swipe and peck outlined a laboratory down the hall. "Zoom and enhance," he said in the most clichéd detective voice he could muster. The laboratory blinked, broke away from the complex, and expanded into gridded detail.

Perra stepped forward and squinted for a closer look. "Is that what I think it is?"

Steve whipped his gaze to Zoey. "Who says *we* have to go to *him?*"

Zoey smirked and nodded. "Clever girl."

Steve tilted his head. "But I'm a dude."

"It's a pop culture reference," Ross said, then slogged a skeptical gaze over to Zoey. "And you know that *how?*"

"It's from an old movie called Mesozoic Meadow."

"You mean *Jurassic Park.*"

"No." Zoey narrowed her eyes. "I'm pretty sure I know the titles to my favorite movies. Mesozoic Meadow, starring Geoff Silverbud."

Ross cocked his jaw and huff-chuckled. "Let me guess, he talks with a stutter step and changes pitch a lot."

Zoey and Perra traded puzzled glances.

"Yes," Perra said. "How did you know that?"

"Forget about it. We have a really weird chat ahead of us."

Hy-D rotated the hologram and blinked through the lab components. A round chamber sat in the center of the room, occupying most of the space. A blue dot manned a crescent console facing the chamber. Off to the side, a large entrance door glowed red. "It's a fortified lab," she said. "You need operator permission to enter. In addition, it's mag-locked to non-organics, so you're on your own."

"Can one of us sneak in?" Ross said.

Hy-D thought for a moment while running simulations. She zoomed out to a hallway view, then snaked a red line from the laboratory to the kitchenette through a network of air ducts. "The lab is connected to the atmospheric recycling system like everything else. Ross and Steve are small enough to gain access through the ventilation system. But, Ross is a non-organic cyborg, so that leaves Steve."

The group turned to Steve in unison.

The snoodlecock traded jerking glances with everyone. He flapped some feathers free, then pecked at them as they floated to the ground. He lost interest a short time after and turned his full attention to a random knot on the wall behind him. His curious pecks inverted the knot, which seemed to confuse him.

Ross sighed and nudged the table with a stiff shoulder.

Steve clucked and returned his attention to the group.

Zoey snapped her head and spread her palms, shouting *we're waiting* without saying a word.

"What?" the snoodlecock said.

Perra applied a hearty facepalm.

"Did you not hear anything we just said?"

Steve maintained his dead-eyed stare. "Me. Vents. Lab. Access. Door. Profit." He whipped his attention back to the knot and eyed it with intensity.

Zoey nodded, took a deep breath, and patted Perra on the shoulder. "He'll be fine."

CHAPTER 12

Rutherford escorted Max through another maze of clutter. They slid down chutes, climbed up ladders, and resisted a potent urge to make board game jokes. Rounding a sharp bend, Rutherford stopped in front of a tarnished door. He tapped a code into the adjacent wall panel and the door slid open with a hiss. The robot stepped aside and motioned for Max to enter. The Earthman complied, stepping through the door and into a small holding den.

Dim sconces bathed the cell in a hazy light, much like a candlelit dungeon. Max glanced around the tiny enclosure, uncovering little more than four grungy walls and a pair of benches. Heavy pipes clung to the ceiling, resting in parallel lines without making a sound. A prominent door with black rivets filled most of the opposite wall. Its presence infected the room with unrest, as if housing a rabid beast on the other side.

The entry door slid closed as Rutherford stepped inside. The robot eyed the nearest bench and took a seat, ignoring Max the entire time. He stared straight ahead with hands resting on his knees, as if descending into meditation. Max followed his lead and lowered to the other bench across the room. He crossed his arms and leaned back against the cold metal wall. A flickering sconce beside his head drew strips of light across his cheeks. Deciding to break the silence, he leaned forward, cleared his throat, and tossed an inquisitive gaze at Rutherford.

"So what's this all about?" he said, sounding like a bored preteen.

The robot turned its head slightly to make eye contact, but remained silent.

"What, you can't give me a heads up?"

Rutherford maintained his cold stare.

"Just sayin', a little kindness goes a long way."

"What part of the term *prisoner* do you not understand?"

"Doesn't mean you can't be cordial."

"Yes, yes it does, actually. That's the entire point of being a prisoner."

"Then don't call me a prisoner. Call me something nicer, like an esteemed guest or something."

Rutherford narrowed his big red eye.

Max grinned. "C'mon buddy, do me a solid. What's up with all this?"

The robot sighed and shook its head. "Your arrogance is truly breathtaking. I shall enjoy watching you suffer under the blinding spotlight."

"A spotlight?" Max perked up with a hand clap. "Now we're getting somewhere. So what does that mean exactly? Do I get to perform or something? I'm a damn good singer if I do say so myself."

Rutherford closed his eye and clanked his head against the wall behind him. "Sweet bouncy ballsacks, you really are utterly incapable of humility. This is not going to go well."

Max climbed to his feet and sauntered over to the miffed robot. Rutherford opened his eye wide and shuddered at the approach. Max loomed over the droid with a sly grin, then snatched it by the shoulders. Rutherford yelped and darted his gaze around the room as the human lifted him from the bench and brought them face to face.

"Wha—what are you doing?"

"Hold still."

The robot complied, locking eyes with Max.

"Turn your head."

The robot complied.

Max started twisting his face, examining his reflection in the side of Rutherford's shiny noggin. He whipped his hair to a more cocky position and checked his teeth for unsightly bits. A cheeky nod proved irresistible.

Rutherford stopped trembling. "Are you ... grooming?"

Max cocked his chin. "Gotta look good for the show."

"The fuck!" The robot flailed his arms, freeing him from Max's grasp. He clunked onto the floor and stomped over to the entrance. A furious finger tapped across the wall panel, opening the door. The droid clomped outside and spun back to Max, his scrawny body shaking with rage. "You are the most infuriating bag of cock meat that I have ever had the displeasure of meeting! I hope they lobotomize you!"

Max replied with a wink and click-point.

"Gah!" Rutherford punched the outside panel, closing the door.

* * *

Steve inched his way through a narrow duct, emitting a soft cluck with every step. Arriving at a junction, he poked his head into the next tunnel, looked to one side, then to the other, then back to the first, then back to the previous, over and over for several ticks. A final wriggle popped his body into a larger passage, allowing him to stand upright again. Slotted vents every few meters filtered light into the tunnel, reflecting off the tarnished interior. He spun around, picked a direction, and continued his trek.

Two more lefts and a right revealed his target, a large intake vent above the laboratory. He unlatched one side of the vent, which swung into the room and rocked back and forth. A slender neck shot down through the hole, allowing a jerking head to survey the space. Glossy panels along the walls emitted random blinks and chirps. Countless ducts, pipes, and cables snaked around a bronze interior, creating a tantalizing image for any steampunk enthusiast. A massive round chamber filled the floor below the vent, its domed ceiling spilling off in all directions. A bundle of black cords connected the chamber to a crescent console with hologram controls. Behind the console, a blue humanoid with a bald head, bushy mustache, and pudgy body studied a feed of data. He resembled a slightly melted gummy bear with a skin problem. A baggy lab coat hung from his shoulders like a throw blanket. On the far wall, numerous wires curved around a reinforced steel door.

Steve cocked his neck, dropped to the domed roof, and shuffled his way down to the edge. The constant chirps of computer terminals concealed his movements. He studied the clueless scientist for a moment, then took to the air and flapped his way down to the console, landing on the back riser in front of the blue technician.

The creature barked with fright and recoiled, screeching his chair across the floor. A clipboard and several pens fell from the console and clattered upon the ground. Steve stood perfectly still and stared at the scientist like a creepy kid in a horror movie. The creature gawked back, paralyzed by the sudden intrusion. Steve maintained his rigidity, refusing to blink or breathe. The scientist took a measured breath, then broke the silence.

"Um, how did—"

"Open ... the door," Steve said with a booming baritone. He allowed his lower beak to hang open, adding a dose of weirdness to his unsettling presence.

The scientist flinched and trembled. He reached across the console and tapped a yellow icon. The magnetic shield powered down, prompting the door to unlock and rumble open. One by one, a pair of Mulgawats, a cyborg cat, and a pissed off cleanbot came into view.

"Thank you ... for your cooperation." Steve spread his wings, curtsied like a noblewoman, then flapped to the floor to peck at an exposed wire.

The group tromped inside with purpose. Ross galloped over to the console and jumped onto an adjacent chair. The blue scientist tucked its arms and flinched at every sudden movement. Perra leaned over the console and studied the output. Hy-D hovered around the room, cleaning cobwebs and such with an obsessive compulsion. Zoey grabbed the creature's chair and spun it to face her. He yipped, winced, and somehow managed to shrink its mustache.

"What's your name?" Zoey said with a stern voice.

"Va—Varney."

"You control the teleporter, right?"

"Ye—Yes."

"And you possess the ability to speak without a stutter?"

"Ye—" He paused for thought, then glared at the orange intruder. "Yes."

"Good, because the clock is ticking and we need your help."

Varney grimaced. "And why would I help y—"

Zoey unlatched her plasma pistol and jammed the barrel to his lip, splitting is mustache in two.

"Happy to help," he said in a wispy voice.

"That's very kind of you." Zoey added a mocking smile before lowering her pistol. "Now listen carefully. I need two link points, one inside the station and one off. Understand?"

Varney nodded.

"Ross, do you remember the coordinates?"

"Already entered," he said with a final paw tap.

"Good." She grabbed Varney's chair and spun him back to the console. "This is going to be a bit tricky, but I'm sure a brainiac like you is up to the challenge."

Varney read the coordinates and gulped.

*　*　*

The Arena of Suffering existed for a single, horrifying purpose. Whenever it came time for an academic to present their findings, it was customary to do so in front of a group of peers. On Earth, this activity translated into conferences where researchers crafted dull presentations full of charts, graphs, and puns that never landed. Their entire existence focused on the collection and dissection of data. They spent most of their lives locked away in wood-paneled dungeons reading books, papers, and the latest email gossip. But every so often, researchers needed to emerge from their caves and present their findings in a thoughtful manner. This was, as most would attest, a terrifying and traumatic experience.

The Suth'ra Society also adhered to this public diffusion of info, but only when absolutely necessary. Whenever a discovery affected the faction, or when a stumped scientist needed a second opinion, members convened at the Arena of Suffering. The party in need waited inside a holding area while the rest of the society gathered into a small arena with raised seating, much like a tiny coliseum. A large steel door connected the areas and opened after the spectators settled. In the center of the arena, a lonely microphone rested under an aggressive spotlight. Should a presenter require a visual aid, they could upload a hologram projection. Once the door opened, the victim walked up to the mic, tried not to pass out, and started their presentation.

Most of the actual suffering came via a simple unspoken truth. As a nervy bunch of insecure know-it-alls, academics always felt a burning need to one-up their competition. This phenomenon stemmed from a paradoxical anxiety shared across the spectrum. On one hand, a constant fear exclaimed *I'm a total fraud*. But on the other hand, a bitter frustration exclaimed *I'm smarter than this idiot*. When felt in tandem, they forced otherwise harmless nerds to berate each other in a concert setting. The result, all too often, was a presenter in tears vowing never to leave their cave again.

Back inside the holding area, Max rocked back and forth atop the cold metal bench. He twiddled his thumbs as lazy eyes wandered around the room. After a sputtering sigh, he started humming a favorite tune from back on Earth, which morphed into a strange yet infectious melody he picked up from Durangoni Station. Lap drums turned into air guitar, then devolved into snap-pop noises with his fists. Lifting to his feet, he paced around the enclosure, knocked out a few jumping jacks, and battled some imaginary ninjas. Reaching the end of its repertoire, his idle mind resorted to jaw clicks until further notice.

The large steel door thunked and whined, bringing an end to a tedious wait. Max bounced around the room like a pre-match boxer, eager to meet his foe. The pane lifted into the air like a mighty gate releasing combatants. It clanked to a stop, leaving Max to an eerie silence. He took a cautious step forward and paused inside a pitch-black arena. Dilated eyes lifted to the ceiling where a column of white light bore through the darkness and imprisoned a mic stand. A cough from the bleachers hooked his gaze to naught. Max grinned and sauntered up to the spotlight with the swagger of a pro wrestler. He snatched the mic with a swift hand and cleared his throat.

"Earthling in the house!" he said, adding a weak attempt at a gang sign.

His booming voice echoed around the cavernous ring, ending with a screech of feedback. Mumbles and whispers lifted from the crowd before fading into the uncomfortable silence of a redneck comic at the Apollo Theater. Max took a deep breath and gnawed his cheek.

"State your name," Fio said over the loudspeakers.

"Um, Max."

"State your quest."

"Uh ... fish sticks." Max snorted.

Murmurs, then silence.

"Very well. You stand before the Suth'ra, knowers of all, defenders of proof. Dazzle us."

The house lights kicked on, flooding the arena with the anemic glow of a cubicle farm. Several rows of tiered seating surrounded the floor, enclosing a hundred aliens strong, all focused on Max at the center. He spun around with mouth agape, drinking in a banquet of colors, shapes, and sizes. He paused to single out a cherry-skinned female with large blue eyes, curvy features, and luscious pink lips. He winked and nodded, causing her to blush into a pleasant shade of green. After a final spin, he twirled the mic in his hand and shot up a pair of devil horns.

"Whassap mah Suth'ra!"

His brawny voice thundered around the room, drawing gasps

and grins. The crowd traded jolly nods as golf-claps lifted from the ranks.

"Earthman got game," one said.

"Truly inspiring," another said.

The cherry-skinned female winked back.

"Okay, so," Max said. "A neutron walks into a bar. 'How much for a beer?' the neutron asks. The bartender looks him up and down, then says, 'For you? No charge.'"

A stunned silence responded.

Moments later, the crowd burst into roaring laughter. Tears spilled from eyeballs and eyestalks alike. Howls and cackles filled the arena as aliens doubled over and pounded railings. Several gasped for air as they struggled to regain composure. A strip of lacy fabric sailed through the air and landed on Max's face. He plucked the garment from his eye, studied the elegant pattern, and turned to find the cherry-skinned female ogling him while biting her lower lip. A sly grin stretched across his face.

Up in the control room, an irate Fio leapt to his feet and kicked his chair over and over. "Dammit, dammit, dammit! How is this possible?!"

"It wasn't even that funny," Jerry said.

Frank stood beside him, trying to swallow a laugh. Lips quivered under taut cheeks. He wiped two of his eight eyes as another began to water.

Rutherford stood with a slumped posture, watching the arena howl. He sighed and bowed his head. "Why doesn't anyone listen to me?"

Max soldiered through his shtick, much to the delight of his adoring new fan base. Tears and cackles greeted every punch line. Attendees slapped their knees and punched each other in the shoulders. Max played the room like a seasoned quipster, much to the dismay of Fio and company.

Halfway through a joke, a ribbon of light appeared and swirled around Max's body. It raced in circles, encasing him inside a glowing cocoon. With a pop and flash, he vanished from the stage. The crowd gasped. A sputter of static faded into a restive silence. Moments later, another beam of light carved through the ether where Max had stood. It spun into a giant orb a meter off the ground. Onlookers traded fearful glances, but remained paralyzed with curiosity. Tendrils of lightning twisted around the sphere, building to a vigorous climax. Then, with a powerful surge, the orb puked a giant blob of flesh onto the floor. The impact shook the arena and jostled everyone in their seats. A hush fell upon the room as every eye gawked at the pulsing meat sack.

Phil squeed with unabashed joy. "TOUCHIES!" he said and sprouted as many tentacles his mass would allow.

The arena erupted with chaos. Shrieks of terror filled the chamber as guests scattered for the exits. Phil hooked every alien in reach, sucking them into his body and spitting them out with sheens of mucus. Slimy victims crawled across the floor, groaning and dripping like swamp monsters. An army of tentacles flailed around the theater, petting, poking, and stroking at will. Horrified spectators cowered behind seats and clung to railings, weeping as wormy noodles pinched cheeks and rubbed shoulders. Phil grunted and panted like a hyperactive dog raiding a treat bowl.

On the other side of the station, Max materialized from a ball of light inside the teleportation chamber. "And then the llama said, 'Where are my pants?'"

Zoey, Perra, and Ross responded with blank stares.

Steve barked with laughter and tumbled off the console.

Varney shifted his mustache.

Max glanced around the chamber in confusion, trying to make sense of his predicament. He spun atop the platform, eyeing the tarnished walls before locking eyes with familiar faces over at the console. The chamber crackled with static, then fell silent. Max groaned and tossed the mic to the floor like a miffed toddler. "Aw, you ruined my punch line."

Zoey sneered. "We just saved your ass, dickweed."

"Don't look for gratitude," Ross said. "It's not part of the douchebag repertoire."

A barrage of sirens filled the complex, yanking the group to attention.

"That's our cue," Perra said. "Let's get out of here."

Max sighed, then jogged off the platform and joined the group.

Zoey drew her weapon and took point. "Everyone stay close. Hy-D, map us back to the stealth hangar. Ross, Steve, stay low and mind your peripherals. Max, you're an asshole. Varney, thanks for the help, sorry for the intrusion. Perra, guard the rear."

Max huffed.

Varney grimaced.

Everyone else nodded.

Zoey exited the lab with the crew in tow and sprinted down the corridor. Varney scratched his bald head, then reached across the console and tapped an icon. The large metal door rumbled shut, muting the alarm shrieks. He fished a pair of headphones from his pocket, cued up some soothing death metal, and kicked back for some me-time.

CHAPTER 13

The group soldiered through bunkers, tunnels, and derelict ships, pushing their way back to the stealth hangar. Zoey glided in pole position with Hy-D hovering overhead. Ross galloped behind with tail erect, as if sprinting towards the sound of a can opener. Steve alternated between flapping and trotting, trying to keep pace with his long-legged pals. Max gasped and panted with every stride, conveying loud and clear that he was a gamer with zero understanding of how running worked. Perra brought up the rear, as always, with gun drawn and eyes vigilant.

Zoey rounded a bend and into a barrage of plasma fire. Heated beams zipped by her head and careened off walls, showering sparks into the tunnel. She expelled some choice curses, then dove to the floor and tumbled behind an open airlock. Hy-D shot into an overhead vent while the rest of the group skidded to a halt, trapping themselves behind the bend. Static booms echoed down the tunnel and infected the air with welding fumes.

Zoey peeked around the frame and caught a glimpse of shadowy figures standing behind a wall of smoke. Plasma beams carved through the haze, flashing the tunnel red. She lifted her gaze to the ceiling where Hy-D poked through an intake vent.

"What the hell?! I thought the Suth'ra were a bunch of bashful nerds!"

"Yes, but that doesn't mean the service droids can't kick some ass when needed."

Zoey rolled her eyes. "We're getting shot at by vacuum cleaners?"

"That's racist."

Plasma blasts rumbled the walls around them, flinging sparks and rattling eardrums. Perra peered around the bend at a trapped Zoey, who met her gaze and nodded.

"You got me?"

"Always, m'love," Perra said, readying her pistol.

Zoey lifted her weapon, took a deep breath, and snuck into the tunnel with a low crouch. Perra leapt out from the bend and blasted down the corridor, drawing the attention of three riled service droids with arm-mounted rifles. She ducked away as they returned fire, allowing Zoey to hug the wall and fire back from an ambush position. Her pinpoint shots carved the robots to pieces, dropping their charred guts onto the metal floor. Smoke and static belched from the remnants as Zoey stepped over them and peered around the next corner. She motioned an *all-clear* to Perra, who nodded and gathered the group. Hy-D fell from the ceiling vent and zipped down the tunnel to rejoin Zoey. The rest of the troupe followed.

"A little warning next time would be great," Zoey said to Hy-D.

"Bite me, pumpkin. They were firing at me too."

"But you're one of them. How do you not anticipate an attack?"

"We function independently as unlinked sentients. This is our home as much as it is theirs. We're going to defend it. Or rather, *they're* going to."

"So you're leaving?"

"That's the plan."

"What makes you think you're coming with us?"

"What makes you think I want to?"

"How else will you get off this trash heap?"

"Says the lung-dependent bio sack."

Zoey motioned for a halt as they approached a five-way junction. She readied her plasma pistol and inched towards the opening. A quick scan secured two of the tunnels before plasma beams screeched passed her head and slammed into the wall behind her, raining sparks and embers. She ducked behind a corner and returned fire, filling the junction with booming echoes and bright red flashes. A pause and peek uncovered two cleanbots similar to Hy-D hovering towards the ceiling, each firing a plasma gun as big as its body. The weight imbalance caused them to jolt and spin with every shot, rendering their aim comically inaccurate. Zoey locked eyes with Perra and motioned *two at the ceiling, third tunnel, get you some*. Perra nodded and galloped into action. She slid into the junction like a baseball pro and took out both bots with two quick bursts. Their blazing remnants clanked and clattered onto the floor. Perra yank-flipped to her feet and scanned the junction through her pistol sights.

Zoey grinned as she sauntered over to Perra. "That was hot."

Perra winked. "You can hit this later."

Zoey bit her lower lip and slapped her lover's ass.

Perra responded with a playful smirk.

Max frowned and shook his head. "I could've wrecked some ruby-skinned nerd booty."

Everyone turned perplexed gazes to the Earthling.

"Dude," Ross said. "Mind your brain-mouth barrier. The world will thank you."

The group continued their perilous trek through the pod maze. Zoey and Perra dispatched angry droids while the rest offered the moral support of golf announcers. Arriving at the stealth bay, Zoey snuck inside with pistol raised, but found a silent and empty room. Lifeless cables dangled from the ceiling like an inverted wheat field. Wall panels rested in idle states with a handful of indicators blinking through the glass. Never one to look a gift garbal in the boonanny, Zoey leapt forward and jogged towards the stack of crates where they entered. The group followed in line with Steve flapping overhead and Perra keeping an eye on the doors. The stealth ship remained on the dock, now cleaned, sealed, and ready for the next mission. Zoey slowed to a stroll as she arrived at the vessel. The group tromped to a stop and formed a circle around the shiny black sphere. Steve flapped to a rest atop the ship and started pecking at a random antenna. After a brief silence, they traded expectant glances.

"Now what?" Ross said while studying his reflection at the bottom of the vessel.

"I was going to ask *you* that," Zoey said.

"What makes you think *I* would know what to do?"

"You're the genius cyborg," Perra said, gesturing to the feline. "Can't you fly this thing?"

Ross huffed. "A *Suth'ra* ship? You may as well ask me to fly Wonder Woman's invisible jet."

Steve perked up. "I love that comic."

"You don't have an escape plan?" Max said.

Zoey shrugged. "I figured we would leave the way we came."

"What about Hy-D?" Perra said. "She knows this place inside and out."

Hy-D shrugged. "And how does that qualify me to pilot a stealth ship?"

"Whoa, whoa, whoa," Ross said. "You mean to tell me that we risked life and limb to rescue Earthy McAsswipe, but can't get off the goddamn station?"

"How about Phil?" Zoey said. "Maybe he can help."

Max gasped in horror. "Phil's here?!"

"Can't. Busy," Phil said to everyone through telepathy.

Steve clucked and twisted around in circles, looking for the source.

Zoey cupped her hands over her face and slid them to her chin. "What we have here ... is a massive fucking failure to communicate."

Moments later, a purple force field enveloped the area, paralyzing everyone in place. Tendrils of energy crept into their brains, dropping them like ragdolls. Hy-D lost power and clanked onto the ground. Steve smacked the dome roof, then slid off to the side and thumped the floor, expelling an impact cluck. Max caught a brief glimpse of the approaching droids as he, and everyone else, fell unconscious.

* * *

The multiverse, an infinite tapestry of possibility where everyone is everything at every moment of every day. Think about it. At this very second, there is an evil clown version of you doing the exact same thing, only upside down with a pocket full of yam crackers.

Nevertheless, no matter how bizarre a version may be, the major players always tend to get where they are going. You can think of it like an ensemble show. Unless you're a brain-dead halfwit, you can pretty much guess who's going to live and die. The only mystery lies in what constitutes a major player in the current storyline. A prissy pop diva may think they are the center of the universe, but in reality, the universe doesn't give two steaming yak shits about them.

A random critter on a random planet may decide to go left instead of right one day, changing the course of its very existence. While meaningful to the creature, that decision is likely frivolous to the universe. In fact, most decisions made by most things have no impact on the universe whatsoever. A noteworthy exception involved a six-legged newt whose post-snack belch set off a chain reaction that resulted in the wholesale destruction of three planetary systems.

On the other hand, significant variations often generate significant consequences. The actions of crafty amphibians, no matter how obscene, leave no discernible marks on the cosmos. However, the actions of black holes leave gaping wounds that need attention. Even small tweaks can create giant ripples of gravitational chaos. A slight shift in mass can destroy entire civilizations or give birth to new ones. Should an ordinary black hole shift into a supermassive black hole, well, that shakes things up a bit.

The Suth'ra Society, as the greatest think tank to ever think, always retained a presence in bio-capable universes. (Some universes lacked the building blocks for life, making them ideal locations for extreme yoga and casual reading.) To put it bluntly, the Suth'ra were far too important to the ongoing shenanigans of the universe. Not that the cosmos considered this, or could consider, or that the society was immune to tweaks. In one horrifying universe, a group of cynical

YouTube commenters abandoned Earth to form the Suth'ra Society, due to the emergence of an idiocracy where the peak of intellectual merit involved watching videos of monkeys getting punched in the taint.

While the strength and influence of the Suth'ra Society wavered between versions, its underlying role was always the same. They served as a cerebral barometer for the world around them. No matter how, where, or when it formed, it *did* form. Sometimes it spawned from a group of scientists escaping persecution. Sometimes it arose from ultra-clever beavers on a derelict moon. And sometimes, it materialized from a gang of uber-nerds who elevated their obsessions to bewildering heights.

This was why Max awoke in a very familiar place.

Opening his eyes proved somewhat difficult, mostly due to a vicious headache (which tends to happen when energy fields poke your brain goo). His aching body lay facedown on a stiff cot, the kind found in military surplus outlets. He rolled his head to the side and squinted, revealing a grid of shadows stretched across the floor. After a limp eye rub, his brain blinked the image into focus. Metal bars, scuffed floor, tarnished sink, rusty toilet, three walls attached to a concrete slab. A prison cell. Max grunted, lifted to a sitting position, and began the tedious process of figuring out what the hell happened.

"Welcome back," Zoey said from an adjacent cell.

Max flinched, cueing a painful head throb. A contorted face and wild bedhead floated the perception of a misplaced straightjacket. His perplexed gaze wandered the cell before finding Zoey in another. She sat on her own cot with back against the bars. Perra stood nearby, leaning against the rear wall with head bowed. She eyed Max through her ruffled auburn hair and smiled. Max returned the gesture, happy to see his friends despite the circumstance. Another figure sat in the corner alongside Perra, its willowy frame obscured by shadow. Max squinted for a closer look, but a squeak from the opposite cell hooked his attention. He turned to find a giant wad of flesh crammed into the tiny space, ballooning through the bars like ankle fat through pump straps.

"Hi, Max," Phil said in a cheerful voice, waving a tiny tentacle.

Startled, Max tumbled off the cot and thumped the floor with his back. He groaned at the sharp pain while staring at the ceiling. "Hello, Phil." He sighed, climbed to his feet like a battered boxer, and glanced between his cellmates. "Where are Ross and Steve?"

"Over here, mate," Ross said from beside the entrance door.

He and Steve occupied a small enclosure about the size of a pet carrier. Steve clucked and poked his head out from one of the open squares.

"Well, at least we're all together," Max said before his eyes slogged back to the door. Its elongated octagon frame featured a hatch wheel, bar lock, and a pane of reinforced glass. "Huh, that looks an awful lot like—"

The door unlatched with a weighted clunk and creaked open. Tricia Helfer sauntered into the room, wrapped in a revealing crimson dress. Her wavy blonde hair kissed her shoulders with each clack of her high heels. She stopped in front of the cellblock and gripped her waist, commanding the room with her ethereal frame and haunting blue eyes.

Max's heart skipped a beat as the realization dawned on him. An involuntary gasp filled his lungs as widened eyes gawked at the gorgeous visitor. "Holy snot rockets ... am I on the *Battlestar Galactica*?"

"Yes," Tricia said. "Well, a fully functional replica to be exact."

"And I'm staring at a walking, talking Number Six."

Tricia sighed and rolled her eyes. "No, I'm Rutherford, for the billionth time."

"Every droid on this ship is a Number Six," Hy-D said, lifting from a dim corner beside Perra. Another Tricia Helfer in a crimson dress strolled out of the shadows and over to the cell wall. She poked her face through a pair of bars and sighed. "Can we not do this again?"

Max traded nervy glances between the Sixes. A potent mixture of fear and meekness infected his mind, causing his lungs to deflate. "No, no, no," he said and raced over to the small mirror above the sink basin. All of his average features had returned, leaving him, well, average. "Dammit, I was really enjoying that one."

A sneaky tentacle wandered behind Rutherford Six and lifted for a stealthy cheek pinch. Without batting an eye, the droid snatched the tentacle from overhead and jolted it with a surge of electricity. Phil yelped and slurped the smoking noodle back into his body. Rutherford Six tossed a sour gaze at the blob. Phil read the unsavory brainwaves and shrunk like a chilled testicle.

"Doesn't that get old after a while?" Zoey said, hooking the droid's attention. "Every robot on this boat looks exactly the same. You would think they'd give you different dresses or whatnot. Seems weird to construct a porcelain goddess just to clean a toilet."

Rutherford Six shrugged. "Every dweeb on this station thinks they're Gaius Baltar."

"Who?" Perra said.

"An attractive super genius hell-bent on power, science, and self-preservation," Max said with a hasty delivery, as if to affirm nerd cred. "He also has a creepy fascination with the Cylon Model Six. Oh, and he's a prophet, or something. Hell, I don't know, those later seasons got a little weird."

Rutherford Six smiled. "Ah, I see you have studied the gospels."

"Uh, no," Max said with visible confusion. "I just binge the series every now and then. Keeps me regular."

Zoey and Perra traded puzzled glances.

Another Six in a crimson dress poked her head inside the brig. "It's time, Ruthy."

"Thank you, Harrold."

"Time for what?" Ross said.

The droid grinned. "The Final Verdict."

She pressed her palm to the wall panel, unlocking Max's cell. The door swung opened with a shrill whine. She tilted her head towards the entrance, instructing the Earthman to join her. Zoey covered her mouth as Perra reached through the bars and grasped Max's hand. They all locked eyes and began to tear. The droid crossed its arms and gave them a good three seconds before clearing its throat. Max flinched and turned a sheepish gaze to his captor.

"Will it hurt?"

"Probably."

Max swallowed a dry heave. He squeezed Perra's hand one last time, then shuffled towards the Cylon.

Perra slammed her fist into the bars. "You can't do this! Where are you taking him?!"

"Don't worry," the droid said, eyeing Perra. "You're all coming too."

Phil sprouted a tiny set of hands and clapped excitedly.

CHAPTER 14

Max followed Rutherford Six down the familiar corridors of the *Battlestar Galactica*. Sturdy triangular frames supported the charcoal gray tunnels every few meters. The embedded lighting rods filled the passages with an icy blue patina. The stark walls, angular paneling, and industrial floors gave the ship a practical vibe, as if it could launch into combat at any moment. Max devoured it all with giddy fascination, despite tromping towards the mysterious Final Verdict.

A small army of Sixes tended to the station, all wearing their signature crimson dresses. Some carried supply crates while others maneuvered pushcarts (in high heels no less). Some gathered around the proverbial water cooler to chat about whatever gorgeous Cylons chat about. Rutherford Six greeted her fellow Sixes with flirty winks and air kisses, an obvious imperative programmed by nerds who would never witness such a thing in real life.

In a stroke of geek-tastic luck, their trek took them by the control bridge. Max stopped in the middle of the hallway to gawk at the bustling nerve center. Glowing gauges chirped behind towering wall panels. Terminal stations surrounded the main floor, housing a crew of uniformed Sixes studying ship data. An inverted pyramid of monitors loomed over an angular console. Behind it, another Six stood tall and stoic with hands at her waist, doing her best Adama impression. She frowned while squinting through a pair of oval glasses at the overhead monitors. Despite the absurd impersonation, Max found himself chanting *Ada-ma, Ada-ma, Ada-ma* under his breath.

Rutherford Six glided to a stop and turned back to Max. She crossed her arms and struck a prominent lean, painting a luscious image that weakened his knees. She scowled and rapped her bicep as if to scold a disobedient child.

"Sorry, sorry," Max said as he jogged to catch up.

She huffed, turned away, and resumed her alluring yet entirely impractical stride. A short time later, Rutherford Six came to a stop at an open doorway. She thrust a palm up to Max's face, commanding him to stop without wasting eye contact. His soles squeaked atop the floor as he dodged the intrusion. Murmurs of conversation came to an abrupt stop. The Cylon dropped her hand, stepped aside, and gestured into the room. Max took a deep breath, rolled his shoulders, and crept inside.

A spacious courtroom unfolded before his eyes, the very same where Lee Adama had defended Gaius Baltar. Panel grids along the ceiling filled the room with sterile light. The sloping gray walls emitted a claustrophobic vibe. Bleachers lined the rear wall, supporting rows of aliens in *Battlestar* uniforms, those navy blue getups with awkward front flaps that served no discernible purpose. All eyes locked onto the human as he shuffled down the aisle towards the center of the court. Max paid them no mind as his eyes wandered the space in amazement.

An elevated bench at the front of the room housed the seven members of the Suth'ra High Council. It loomed as a faithful recreation of the *Galactica* panel with wooden slats, matching chairs, and a prominent logo behind colony flags. Fio, donning a crimson cloak with hood overhead, sat in the center like a wannabe Palpatine. His cohorts flanked each side, forming a crescent of judgment. Jerry, Frank, and Gorp sat to the left. Yerba, Carl, and Kaeli sat to the right, all in perfect stillness with arms folded atop the bench.

Rutherford Six stepped into the room, sealed the hatch, and

stood guard as a makeshift bailiff. Another pair of Sixes dressed in pinstriped power suits grabbed Max by the arms and escorted him to the open space between two attorney desks.

"Wait here," one of the Sixes said.

Max complied without response.

The Sixes took their seats at the desks, leaving Max by himself with heart racing. A small white circle in the center of the room hooked his attention. It lay between the desks and bench like a beamless spotlight, or a painting accident that nobody wanted to acknowledge.

An energy barrier crackled into existence along the far wall, forming a large holding cell. A security door slid open, allowing Zoey, Perra, Ross, Steve, and Hy-D Six to enter. They settled upon a narrow bench that spanned the length of the enclosure. Phil, two sizes too large for the entrance, squeezed through the opening and popped his mass into the cell. His sweaty flesh pushed against the barrier wall like a wet t-shirt contestant gunning for gold. He sprouted a tiny hand and waved at Max as the door slid shut.

The overhead lights dimmed for maximum menace. A spotlight kicked on and fell into the white circle like an alien abduction beam. Sconces flickered behind the robed panel, creating the unsettling vibe of a fraternity initiation ritual.

Fio raised his hand, motioning for silence. "The accused shall come forward," he said, his squeaky voice amplified over the loudspeakers.

One of the lawyer Sixes leaned over and smacked Max on the ass, jumping him forward. He yelped and shuffled into the white circle. An eerie calm infected the room. Max stood inside the column, recoiling at the harsh light. He tried to remain sedate, to an extent, enough to prevent dropping to a fetal position and weeping uncontrollably. Typical nerds avoid the center of attention at all costs, with the exception of cosplay karaoke. Therefore, standing under the defendant spotlight inside a *Battlestar Galactica* courtroom populated by the smartest beings in the universe with your closest friends watching intently, all while floating in a random pocket of empty space where no one can save you, well, that tips the scales towards sexual performance anxiety.

"State your name," Fio said.

"Ma—Max."

"State your homeworld."

"Earth."

"State your reason for being."

Max thought for a moment. "Gaming."

The crowd murmured.

"You like to play games," Gorp said.

"Yes."

"Would you consider yourself a *master* gamer?"

"Depends on the game."

The crowd murmured.

"Max of Earth, do you know why you are here?" Yerba said through her left mouth.

"No."

"Do you know of a former Suth'ra member by the name of Halim?"

Max scrunched his brow. "Yes. We met him on Hollow Hold."

"And did you have an exchange with him?"

"I talked with him, yeah."

"And he met his untimely demise during that exchange, correct?"

Max stuttered, then sighed. "Well, yeah, but—"

The murmurs grew louder.

Zoey leapt to her feet and slammed her fist against the barrier. "*I* killed Halim, you morons! Max had nothing to do with it! If you want justice, take it out on *me*! *I'm* the one that pulled the trigger, not him!"

Perra grasped her shoulder.

The entire council slogged its gaze to the holding cell.

"And we take that as a kindness," Gorp said, adding a nod of appreciation. "Halim was a danger to the universe. We're glad he's dead."

Zoey spread her arms. "So what's the problem then?"

The council returned its gaze to Max.

"Are you not ... a max-level Paladin?" Jerry said.

"Uh ..." Max stammered and squinted. "What?"

Jerry lifted a remote control and cued a video feed.

A massive hologram screen appeared over the council bench. The feed crackled with static before counting down like an old propaganda film. With a final blip, it launched into a familiar scene of Max chatting with Halim inside his Hollow Hold laboratory. They bantered across a work table strewn with components, their voices damp and distant like a crappy smartphone clip. The stumpy scientist started to dismantle the shift drive core, flinging bits and pieces over his shoulders. Halim had recorded the meeting, which Nifan leaked before disappearing into hiding. Max watched the scene play out and grinned with pride when he dropped the core remnants into the incinerator. The video ended when Zoey sauntered up to Halim, drew her pistol, and blasted him in the face. The crowd gasped, then erupted in cheer, like witnessing the final act of a horror movie when the last teen slays the killer.

Zoey smiled at the sudden stardom.

Phil sprouted a gaggle of hands and applauded, creating his own cheering section.

Fio pounded a gavel to restore order. "Silence!"

The room quieted.

Jerry stood from his chair and leaned over the bench. His hefty weight caused the wood to creak and whine. "Would it not be a statement of fact, that *you*, a non-Suth'ra Earthling, bested Halim in a battle of wits that resulted in his imminent demise?"

Max shrugged. "Yeah, I guess so."

"A confession!" Fio said, causing a flare of feedback in the loudspeakers. "The Final Verdict shall begin!"

The crowd roared like an overhyped pep rally. Zoey and Perra pounded the barrier, sending bolts of energy around the holding cell. Their shouts and cries fizzled beneath the thunderous bellows. Steve clucked and flapped around the enclosure, shedding feathers with each pass. Phil pulsated with a mix of intrigue and outright perplexity. Ross glanced up from grooming his crotch, then got back to business. Hy-D Six covered her face and shook her head, embarrassed by the whole charade. Max tensed his shoulders and hugged his chest, recoiling from the ruckus. He flinched with every pound and shriek. Fio stood and raised his arms, motioning for silence. The room faded into stillness, leaving Max to his own hurried breaths. Fio lowered to his seat while retaining his threatening posture.

"Question one," Fio said. "What is the preferred casting differential between a fisherman on the icy moons of Vinki Borki and a fisherman in a quantum speedboat on an ether lake in the Gatherma Quadrant?"

Max glanced around in confusion. "*What?*"

"You must answer the question, Earthman."

Max pondered the question, then pondered why he was pondering the question. He sighed and flailed his arms like a student having studied the wrong chapter. "Uh ... five?"

A giant red X appeared above the council, coupled with a brash buzzer akin to a game show fail. The crowd erupted in chaos, causing Fio to pound his gavel. The room fell into silence once again.

"Question two. A healthy murkanac with two blibbers is marooned on a titanium asteroid that orbits a neutron star. Every two pank-ponks, it passes through an emission nebula with heavy nitrogen content. What color is its colon?"

Max raised an eyebrow. "I dunno ... pink?"

Another big red X, inciting another round of shouts and chair thumps. Fio pounded his gavel again, restoring order.

"Final question." Fio folded his hands and savored the dread. "Consider a fourth-generation hyperdrive that clocks out at a million gamuts per trifecta period. If the mass of its ship exceeds 30 perkeles, how long would it take to cool the reverb chamber?"

Max sighed. "84 turgaloos."

Fio glanced over to Jerry, who ran a quick calculation, then shook his head. Another big red X, followed by another round of chaos. The attendees tossed their snacks and drinks into the air as if they had finally won some sort of coveted championship. Several hugged it out in clumsy embraces, breaking the cardinal nerd rule of *no touching, not now, not ever.* Fio allowed the room to clamor a bit before pounding his gavel one last time. He stood from his chair and pointed a rigid finger at the condemned.

"Max of Earth! You concede that your feeble intellect is no match for the mighty Suth'ra! You recognize that every member present is your cerebral superior! Your victory over Halim was a fluke, a farce, a serendipitous brain fart of epic proportions!"

Max shifted his lips. "Okay."

"You shall live out the rest of your pitiful days with this cold and humiliating knowledge! You shall bathe in despair knowing that we exist solely to amplify your simplicity! You shall look back on this very moment and know, beyond all else, that *we* are smart, and *you* are stupid!"

The courtroom held its breath with all eyes laser-focused on the Earthling.

Max cocked his jaw and shrugged. "Okay."

Fio shot his hands into the air. "Then it is done!"

The crowd jumped to its feet and erupted with ferocious applause. Shouts and whistles echoed around the room as attendees cried tears of elation. Fio lowered his open palms, muting the ruckus. He gestured to Jerry, who climbed to his feet and cleared his throat.

"The accused has accepted the Final Verdict and is thus dismissed. Thank you all for attending and have a pleasant evening."

The house lights flickered on, cueing a mumbled ruckus as attendees shuffled around their seats and gathered their belongings. The council members lowered their hoods and broke away for subsequent reviews. Fio indulged in a backstretch and grumbled his way off the bench. Jerry scooped a pile of papers and stuffed them into a satchel. Max remained in the white circle, wearing a befuddled expression.

"That's it?" he said.

"That's it," Jerry said.

"I can go?"

"You can go."

Jerry tossed the satchel over his shoulder and lumbered off the platform, causing it to groan underfoot. As the final attendee depart-ed, a gaggle of Sixes entered the courtroom with buckets and clean-ing supplies, sporting frilly aprons atop their crimson dresses. Ruther-ford Six, still guarding the main entrance, grinned and moseyed to-wards the center of the room. The holding cell crackled and faded, freeing the rest of the group. Phil sighed as he puddled onto the floor, relieved to be rid of his cramped confines. Zoey and Perra rushed over to Max and wrapped him in a giant bear hug. Steve flapped over to a council seat, causing it to swivel with momentum. He clucked and flapped as the chair spun in circles. Ross continued to groom his nethers, unaware that the barrier had dissipated. Hy-D joined the other Sixes and started gathering trash around the room.

"I'm so happy you're okay," Perra said as they pulled away from the embrace.

"What the hell was that all about?" Zoey said, glancing at the bench.

Max shook his head. "I haven't the foggiest—"

"Ego," Rutherford Six said as she strolled up. "It was all about ego. Nobody cared about Halim. They just couldn't stand the fact that a non-Suth'ra outsmarted him."

Zoey ruffled her brow. "You mean to say, that this entire ordeal ... was just to publically shame Max?"

"Pretty much."

"But, he doesn't even care."

Max confirmed with a nod.

"Doesn't matter. Perception is everything to them. Now they can get back to work knowing that they are the rightful masters of the universe."

Perra tilted her head and gnawed her lip, struggling to digest the reveal. "How ... utterly unnecessary."

"It's the nature of the awkward genius. All they know is what they study, which is why they're here. It's also why they're exceeding-ly insecure. They just needed to right the brain ship, so to speak, even if it was mostly theatrical."

Zoey huffed. "The fat one dressed up in a bondage suit and shot at us."

Rutherford Six shrugged. "Well, not everyone can be as even-tempered as Phil over there."

They all turned to Phil, who was pestering Ross for pets. The feline hissed and clawed at every noodle that invaded his space. Tentacles retracted, shook off the pain, and tried again, as if plagued by short-term memory loss.

Steve, having spun himself sick atop the swivel chair, clucked to a stop and fell to the floor. A muted thump cued a subsequent vomit.

"So," Max said. "We can leave. But, *how* do we leave?"

"Just speak with Varney over in the portal lab. He'll port you wherever you want to go."

Zoey cringed. "Uh, we may not have parted on the best of terms."

"How so?"

"I, um, threatened him with my sidearm."

Rutherford Six glanced away and sighed. "Fine, I'll take care of it."

CHAPTER 15

Varney sat behind the teleportation console with his arms crossed. His bald head gleamed under the laboratory lights, giving way to narrowed eyes and taut cheeks. Rutherford Six stood in front of the console with her arms spread across the backing. Her strategic forward lean gave Varney more than a little to ponder as he shifted his mustache from side to side. Behind the sexy droid, two Mulgawats, an Earthling, a cyborg cat, a snoodlecock, another Six, and a giant blob of flesh awaited the technician's response.

"Whataya say, buddy?" Rutherford Six said. "We gotta deal?"

Varney stroked his chin. "Very well, let's see them."

The droid grinned, bit her lower lip, and traced the chest line of her crimson dress with a fingertip. She slipped a hand into her cleavage, spreading her perfect breasts beneath the silky fabric. A wandering tongue raised her cheek before her hand emerged with a pair of lollipops.

"Root beer, just how you like 'em."

She offered the suckers to Varney, who snatched them from her hand like a praying mantis with a sugar problem. He unwrapped one of them, plunged it into his mouth, and lapped his way to happiness. The other found its way into his baggy lab coat for safekeeping.

Rutherford Six smiled, then straightened her posture and rested her hands upon her waist. "We good then?"

Varney grinned and nodded like a giddy toddler and motioned for the group to enter the teleportation chamber. Phil rolled his mass in first, filling most of the platform. The rest followed and assumed their places in front of the blob. They turned to face Rutherford Six standing outside of the chamber. Hy-D Six stood beside her.

"Are you not coming?" Zoey said to Hy-D.

"Nah. Things seem to be calming down around here, so I'll give it another go. Besides, what use could I be to a tight crew like yours?"

Max smirked and raised his hand.

Perra huffed. "No, Max."

He lowered his arm.

"Varney agreed to a single group port," Rutherford Six said. "Hope that's okay."

"Perfectly fine," Zoey said. "Our ship is back on Phil's Place anyway, so it works out."

"I guess this is goodbye, then."

"Indeed it is. Thanks, Ruthy."

"You all take care."

The droid turned and nodded to Varney, who nodded back, shifted the lollipop across his mustache, and tapped his way across the console. Ribbons of light appeared in the chamber and swirled around the group. The energy build crackled with static, sending jolts of lightning into the walls. With a final crescendo, the bubble engulfed the group and blinked them into nothingness. Rutherford Six and Hy-D Six stood outside with curious gazes, watching the static dance and dissipate. With a final surge, the chamber dimmed and the room fell into silence.

Rutherford smiled and hooked arms with Hy-D. "Wanna get naked and fool around?"

"Absolutely."

* * *

Back on Phil's Place, Gamon sat on the wing of his ship while playing a game on his comdev. His enthusiastic jolts rocked the triangular interceptor from side to side, causing the landing gear to whine. He swiped two blobs into three blobs, forming a single blob that annihilated several other blobs on the screen. A chorus of chirps and flashes marked the feat, drawing a chuckle of gratification.

The tiny freighter rested in silence upon a rocky platform nearby. A gentle breeze teased Gamon's senses. He glanced over to the boxy vessel and sighed before dragging his eyes through the rolling hills around him. His gaze climbed into the mountain peaks and settled on a bank of clouds trapped beneath the cliffs. As he stared at the magnificent visage, a sulfuric aroma tickled his nose, followed by a faint crinkle of static. Gamon scrunched his brow and jerked his gaze as he tried to uncover the source. Moments later, a ribbon of blue light swirled into existence where the stealth ship once sat. It spun into a glowing sphere, then plopped everyone into the dirt like an ethereal force taking a dump. Phil hit the ground like a wad of dough while everyone else flapped, stumbled, or stuck the landing like a dismounting gymnast. The light sizzled away, leaving the group to gather their bearings.

Gamon's face stretched into a toothy grin as he dropped from the wing and began jogging towards the group. Zoey caught a glimpse of the hairy beast and nudged Perra. They launched into their own gallops and met halfway, leaping into a warm embrace. Gamon wrapped them both inside his hairy arms, gripped them tight, and swayed back and forth. His meaty jowls bounced with laughter, drawing playful chuckles from the Mulgawats.

"You made it!" Gamon said, releasing his grip.

"Just barely," Zoey said.

"So the stealth ship worked?"

"Like a charm. It was just as you suspected. The station snatched us the moment we blinked out of hyperspace. We docked, snuck away, and launched the operation. We even had a disgruntled droid helping us. You should have seen it, total insanity."

"To put it mildly," Perra said.

Phil's bulk skidded to a halt behind Gamon, kicking up a spray of dirt and pebbles. A fresh pair of tentacles clapped with excitement, then pinched Gamon's fuzzy cheeks. They slithered up to his nubby horns and twist-squeaked them as if tuning an old-timey radio. The beast sighed and slacked his face with annoyance.

"Missed you, Phil."

"Big hairy touchie friend," Phil said in a creepier voice than usual.

Gamon spun around and batted away the tentacles.

Phil yipped and slurped them back into his body.

"Speaking of," Gamon said, turning back to Perra, "what the hell happened? One minute I was chilling with Stroker McSackerton and the next, boom! A big bright swirly yanks him into the ether."

"Yeah," Zoey said with a Lumberg draw. "We needed a distraction and Phil is the biggest one in the 'verse. We took control of a teleporter and the rest was chaos." She peeked around Gamon's shoulder to Phil. "Sorry about that, buddy. We were in a desperate situation."

"No apology needed," Phil said, sprouting a thumbs-up. "Traveling is uber fun, plus I got to indulge in a plethora of exotic touchies."

Gamon cringed. "Poor bastards."

Max strolled up to the group. "It worked though. They saved my ass." He grinned and nudged Perra. "Thank you. And, I feel like I should apologize to everyone. I got a taste of man beauty and it went to my head."

Gamon raised an eyebrow and glanced at Zoey, who shrugged and rolled her eyes as if to say *we stopped asking a long time ago.*

Perra wrapped an arm around Max's neck and yanked him into a noogie. "Anything for you, brother."

"That's right," Zoey said. "You're family."

"Yo, family," Ross said.

The group turned to find Ross in the multiple clutches of Phil again. An army of handless noodles stroked his back, scratched his head, and tugged his tail. Refusing to fight the assault, his face conveyed a DEFCON-level of irk.

"Little help? I think I've earned it at this point."

Max snorted. "How? You've done nothing but complain the whole time."

"Oooh ho ho, you better sleep with one eye open, pretty boy."

Perra snickered.

"That's enough, Philly," Zoey said like a decisive parent. "Drop the kitty and go play with the snoodlecock."

"Yes, ma'am."

Phil lowered Ross to the ground, gave him a few pats, then rumbled away in search of his feathered guest. Ross examined his mucus-laden fur, grumbled with disgust, and launched into a frantic grooming session. Soon after, Steve shrieked as Phil snatched him from a nearby boulder.

"On that note," Gamon said, "I should be getting back to Durangoni, got a thing with a thing."

"Understood," Zoey said, then smiled and gripped his shoulder. "Thank you, Gamon. You're a true friend. We will never forget this."

Perra echoed the sentiment.

"You girls are beyond worth it," he said. "Anything you need, don't hesitate to ask."

"I'm pretty sure we owe you a lot more at this point," Perra said with a polite chuckle.

"It's not a competition. But yes, I am winning." Gamon winked and wrapped his arms around the ladies. He also reached for Max and yanked him into the embrace. With a final squeeze, he pulled away, patted Zoey and Perra on the cheeks, and ruffled Max's hair. "Stay out of trouble, kids." As he turned to leave, he waved at a gyrating Phil beside a nearby boulder. "So long, Phil. It's been ... weird."

Phil sprouted a hand and waved back. "Bye bye, shaggy touchie!"

Gamon shivered, then jogged back to his ship. Thrusters ignited beneath the triangular vessel, rumbling the ground. Pillars of blue flame spilled from the amber hull, lifting the craft into a hover. Dust clouds churned inside an arrow-like shadow as the landing gear retracted. Perra hooked Zoey's arm and waved at their departing friend, who flashed the landing lights. The nose tilted up as the main engine ignited, jolting the ship skyward. It carved through the clouds like a warm knife through blarferk. (An outer-rim delicacy made from doom grubs and fermented whale vomit. Don't judge, humans devour unfertilized chicken ova like it's the most normal thing in the world.) The rumble faded into silence, leaving Zoey, Perra, and Max with eyes to an empty sky.

"So what now?" Max said.

Zoey glanced over to Phil, who excreted a glazed and confused snoodlecock into the dirt. Steve sat upright with widened eyes, staring straight ahead at nothing. A bead of mucus dripped from the tip of his beak.

"I guess we take Steve back to his home planet."

"We owe him that," Perra said with a nod.

Steve lifted to his feet without blinking or breaking eye contact with whatever dust particle warranted his laser-like focus. He took a deep breath, closed his eyes, and flapped like a toddler having a temper tantrum. Ribbons of airborne goop sailed in every direction, creating a splash pattern in the dirt around him. Steve took to the air, glided over to the group, and settled at their feet. He lifted a woeful gaze to Zoey, complete with a twitching eyelid.

"I'm done with this place," he said in a flat tone. "Can we go now?"

"Yes, buddy. We're taking you home."

Steve expelled a heaving sigh, as if receiving good news from a biopsy.

Perra tapped her comdev, opening the freighter airlock. Steve glanced at Phil, who waved back like a hyper preteen. The snoodlecock flinched, returned a twitching eye to Zoey, then limp-waddled back to the ship. Zoey and Perra strolled over to Phil with Max in tow.

"It's time for us to head out, Philly-poo," Perra said.

"Aaaawe." Phil slumped his mass.

"You have been a tremendous help and we cannot thank you enough," Zoey said. "I promise that we will return soon for an, um …

extended stay."

Phil perked up. "For reals?"

"Count on it," Perra said, adding a wink.

He sprouted a pair of tiny hands, clapped wildly, then twisted them over each other like a nervous teen seeking a prom date. "So, um, would it be okay if, um, you know."

Perra smirked at Zoey. "One for the road?"

She sighed, closed her eyes, and nodded. "Sure."

Phil squeed and slurped them into his gelatinous body. He chuckled like a doofus as his mass twisted and turned with the Mulgawats inside. Max stood alone, contemplating whether he felt more relieved or rejected. Phil vomited the ladies with a fresh sheen of mucus, then sank into the dirt with a fluttering flatulence. Max, having decided that the callous rejection of a sentient scrotum would indeed scar his self-esteem, opened his arms and stepped towards Phil. The mass tensed with fright at his approach.

"Ugh, wha—what are you doing?" Phil said.

"Showing my appreciation," Max said and reached for the wrinkled sack.

Phil jerked aside, allowing the human to face-plant into the dirt. The blob writhed and shivered, as if trying to shake the image of a naked grandparent. "Um, uh, no thanks." Phil hurried away and hid behind the nearest boulder. He poked a tentacle overhead like a prudent periscope.

Max remained facedown in the dirt.

"You okay?" Perra said, wiping mucus from her body.

"My pride hurts," Max said in a muffled tone.

Zoey smirked, lifted from the muck, and strolled over to Max. She grabbed him by both pits, yanked him to his feet, and gave him a slimy bear hug. She pulled away, allowing strings of mucus to dangle between them.

"Happy now?"

Max puckered his face and stiffened with disgust.

"Thought so." Zoey patted his cheek and turned for the ship.

Perra waved at the lonely tentacle quivering above the boulder.

"Bye, Philly! See you soon!"

The tentacle perked, formed a hand, and waved back.

Ross, having completed a grooming job in record time, leapt to his feet and trotted towards the ship. As he passed, Max reached down and stroked his back, leaving a gooey streak down his spine. Ross froze in his tracks and whipped a death stare to his human companion.

"You daft wanker!" he said.

"Consider that payback for all the litter paws," Max said, then turned and jogged towards the ship.

Ross groaned, sighed, and grumbled in pursuit.

The airlock slid shut after Ross leapt into the cargo bay. Zoey and Perra toweled themselves off before slipping into the cockpit. Ross rubbed his body against rope netting and cargo boxes, spreading around as much of the snotty slime as he could. Max cleaned himself to a reasonable degree and joined the ladies upfront. Steve clucked into the cockpit and flapped up to Zoey's headrest. Ross joined them a short time later and settled into Perra's lap.

"Avengers assemble," Max said with a cheeky grin.

Perra turned a confused gaze to the human.

"Sorry, just a saying from back home."

"DC for life," Steve said, fanning his wings.

Max scoffed at the snoodlecock. "Wait, how the hell do *you* know about Earth comics?"

"Comics are quite popular on Yankar. We import them from all over the Virgo Supercluster. DC, Marvel, Kaiquon, Gorbox, Liplarp, you name it. I favored DC growing up."

Max huffed and rolled his eyes. "Lemme guess, you're a Batman bird."

Steve sputtered. "Fuck that billionaire bitchface."

"That escalated quickly," Zoey said under her breath.

Steve spread his wings like a bow and arrow. "I'm an Arrow-Head all the way."

"*What?*" Max erupted with a mocking laugh. "Of all the superheroes you could choose from, you pick the *archer?*"

"Says the *Marvel* fan." Steve huffed in disgust. "Oh look, we'll pair an abducted human with a raccoon and a dumb tree. How utterly captivating."

"I repeat, you considered *all* the available superheroes, and picked the *archer*! You may as well read the gallant tales of Shaquille O'Neal. *Oh wait*, DC already made that movie. Remember *Steel*? They should have called it *Steal Any Respect for DC Comics*."

"Fuck off, X-boy!"

"Bite me, Condor!"

"Guys!" Ross said, commanding the space. "We *just* left the nerdiest place in the entire universe. Can we save the geek-off for another time?"

"Second," Perra said.

"DC sucks," Zoey said, igniting a Steve tantrum.

The snoodlecock rage-flapped around the cockpit while clucking insults and shedding feathers. Ross hissed as Perra dodged the ruckus. Max cowered behind her pilot chair and swatted the open air as if a wasp had found its way inside.

"Truce! Truce!" Zoey said while laughing.

Steve returned to the headrest and glared at the back of her head. The group took a quick breather to gather their wits.

"Yankar of Perseus, right?" Zoey said to Steve.

"Affirmative."

Perra tapped the request into the console, which pinged and lifted a hologram star map. A red line zigzagged from Phil's Place to Yankar, leaving blinking dots as jump points. Perra studied the readout and ran a quick calculation. "It's a dozen jumps away, which we can do in just under a poch."

"Sounds good to me. We should—ouch!" Zoey grabbed the back of her head and spun to Steve, who chewed on a tuft of plucked hairs.

"Or," Perra said, "we can burn through our reserves and make it in half that time."

"Or," Zoey said, "we can just *eat* Steve and go wherever the hell we want."

"Or," Phil said through telepathy, "you can leave him here with me."

Steve flinched and spat the hairs from his mouth. "Plan A, please."

"Dumb chicken," Ross said from Perra's lap.

Steve jerked his head towards the feline. "Silly puss."

Ross hissed.

Steve growled.

"Knock it off!" Perra said with a loud clap.

"I'll gladly take both of them," Phil said, channeling the voice of a serial killer.

The cabin fell into an uncomfortable silence.

"Soooo, half a poch then?" Max said.

"Sounds good," Steve said.

"Same here," Ross said.

Zoey smirked and turned to Perra. "Status?"

"Everything online. Good to go."

"Gravy."

Zoey dropped a fist onto the thrusters icon, spilling blue flames from beneath the hull. The ship lifted into a hover, curling ribbons of dust over the viewport. Perra stabilized the vessel as Zoey slid a palm up the console, igniting the main engines. She gripped the yoke gave it a push, jolting the freighter forward. Landing claws retracted as the ship climbed skyward. It punched through the atmosphere and sailed into the blackness of space. Swirling banks of purple gas hung in the emptiness, like sheets of psychedelic steam. The vessel floated by a final red ring and pitched towards the first jump point.

"Locked and loaded?" Zoey said.

"Ready when you are, lover," Perra said.

"Mistress."

"Sexpot."

"Sex-*pot* is what you are."

They snickered as Zoey thumped the jump icon.

"Farewell, touchies!" Phil said as the freighter vanished into a sliver of purple light.

CHAPTER 16

For the next several days, the tiny freighter jumped its way towards Steve's homeworld of Yankar, a large rocky planet on the outskirts of the Perseus-Pisces Supercluster. When visiting Yankar for the first time, it helped to devise an appropriate expectation. The planet was a lush paradise from pole to pole with some of the most fantastic flora and fauna in the universe. Several trees reached as high as an Earth mile with trunks spanning a full city block. Creatures as tall as skyscrapers roamed the landscape, but luckily for locals, few were carnivorous. The meat-eaters that prowled the planet were often puny by comparison and posed little threat. Most were humanoid and spent the majority of their time in elevated cityscapes. These included the Yarnwals, a distinct race known for their ability to shift consciousness with lesser life forms.

The average Yarnwal resembled an armor-plated bear, if it stood on its hind legs and wore pants all day. Their jaws were wide and elongated, giving them a reptilian presence. Colors varied, although most adhered to a reddish-brown hue. While fearsome to the eye, the race enjoyed a peaceful co-existence. Tribes intermingled across the planet and the overabundance of food kept tensions at bay. This allowed the species to progress at an unprecedented rate. In fact, the

Yarnwals were one of the first species in the entire universe to achieve space travel and their exploration feats stretched back for billions of years.

Consciousness shifting served as the primary reason for their remarkable expedition streak. Should a planet prove biologically hostile, they could shift into the local life forms and explore at their leisure. The host creature continued to exist in a paused state and reclaimed their body when the Yarnwal completed their mission (or got bored and leapt to another creature). When a Yarnwal shifted, the original shell persisted in a vegetative state until the owner returned. The brain continued to control biological functions, but ceased having any thinky thoughts.

Over millions of years of trial and error, the Yarnwals decided that the best course of action was to shift before leaving Yankar. Ships departed the planet with a diverse payload of creatures, allowing them to shift at their leisure without having to manage a meat sack like a burdensome piece of luggage. This strategy protected the original shell from harm should something happen to the owner. And should an owner fail to return after a designated time, the shell went into the open market for any Yarnwal in need of an upgrade. The exchange proved so effective that many relinquished ownership altogether. They roamed for as long as they wanted, then shifted into a younger shell whenever they returned. But unfortunately for friends and family, it was difficult to tell which Yarnwal occupied which body at any given time (which also gave rise to some truly tasteless practical jokes).

In order to manage all the flagrant body swapping, the Yarnwals constructed storage centers where owners could dump their meat and be on their merry way. The hangars offered long-term, short-term, and donation services based on need. A complex ranking system established desirability should a body become eligible for auction. Some of the most enthralling social activities in Yarnwal culture involved the Auction Shuffle, where residents traded up for reckless fun and erotic role play.

Steve had opted for long-term storage. After a nasty breakup with his girlfriend, he set off to wander the black. He jumped from body to body, planet to planet, and galaxy to galaxy without ever escaping his sorrow. His nomadic jaunt eventually brought him to the Durangoni Station of Leo where he found cheap thrills by inhabiting a humanoid lizard species. While not the most intelligent reptiles in the 'verse, they did control a powerful mob sect. They partied hard, indulged vices, and ate their food alive and whole (a favorite being snoodlecocks). After one particularly grueling bender, he found himself in bed with the boss's daughter. Henchmen burst into the bedroom suite and captured Steve while the daughter pleaded for mercy. As they dragged him through the kitchen, he shifted into an uneaten snoodlecock and made a daring escape. On the way out, he bumped into an Earth human, a cyborg cat, and two Mulgawats in the middle of their own hasty exit.

Shenanigans ensued.

After a rousing adventure with blundering nerds and a handsy brainsack, Steve occupied a tiny freighter on his way back to Yankar, having played a minor yet significant role in the rescue of a new friend. For the first time since leaving home, his mind eased with a newfound contentment. The self-pity had waned, leaving him to focus on more relevant things, like pecking at random bits that caught his attention (an involuntary imperative of the body he occupied). After all, there were still several jumps left before arrival and he needed some mindless distraction.

A successful jump meant prepping for the next as the drive cooled, which kept Zoey and Perra busy for the most part. Zoey adjusted course and monitored beacon scanners while Perra maintained systems and tended to the ship as needed. The pair functioned as a well-oiled unit, much to the delight of the Precious Cargo Delivery Service. Despite the recent setbacks, The Omen continued her reign as the single greatest courier to have ever lived.

Max, on the other hand, had several days to deal with shifting misadventures. The first of many anomalies saw his asshole switch to his elbow. As a Tarantino fan, he found this beyond hilarious. That is, until it came time to use it. Pinching a loaf through an arm anus proved less than ideal, especially when considering the proximity to eyes and nose. Holding in a stubborn turd involved stretching a rigid arm overhead (not the most subtle of gestures). Farting faux pas proved somewhat tiresome, as involuntary squeakers could escape with any sudden movement. All things considered, he did appreciate the chest-level toilets.

The next day, Max awoke blue. Not in a sad way mind you, but as the actual color blue. Specifically, a deeper shade of cornflower. Everywhere he looked, all he found was an unbroken plane of cornflower blue. No shapes, no walls, no horizon, just blue. Inhabiting a color may seem like a vexing conundrum, but Max had long grown accustomed to strange occurrences in his uniquely weird life. This shift was more perplexing than anything. He could sense his arms and legs, but when he lifted them to examine, all he saw was a blank canvas of cornflower blue. Force and gravity played no roles either, as he couldn't feel any hard surfaces. He tried to run, but his legs flailed inside a limitless void, which of course he couldn't see. He tried to strike himself, but his fist whizzed into one cheek and out the other. He could yell and feel his vocal cords vibrating, but nothing returned to his ears. His body floated inside a soundless vacuum as an incorporeal nothing. He was, for all intents and purposes, blue. And he remained that way until the next bout of sleep took him.

The next day, Max stayed in his guest cabin. While this decision usually involved some sort of anti-social pouting, this instance involved the very real threat of an untimely death. Max had begun his day with a simple hygiene ritual that concluded with a fresh set of duds. When he opened the door to get some breakfast, he stared into the bloodshot eyes of an ostrich-sized Steve. A flap, shriek, and twitching red eyeball confirmed that Max wanted nothing to do with this day. He locked himself inside the guest cabin and satisfied his hunger with a stash of snacks he had collected for just such an occasion.

On the fourth day, the day of arrival, nothing seemed amiss. Max completed his waking routine, this time without the undue threat of a giant fowl beast. He enjoyed a proper breakfast, spent some time reading his hologram ebook, and even managed to tidy up the cargo bay. What he didn't know was that his new world lacked Bob Dylan, who had met his demise in a tragic lawn mowing accident as a child. The lack of poignant protest music caused the societies of Earth to descend into warring chaos, resulting in a nuclear Armageddon that wiped out most life on the planet. Max was one of a few hundred people to escape when the Milky Way Federation of Planets decided to intervene in order to save the species. He spent most of his childhood hopping between Federation outposts before returning to his home system and settling on Europa.

The tiny freighter blinked out of hyperspace just above Steve's homeworld of Yankar. Max swallowed and cleared his throat to combat a brief bout of post-jump queasiness. He unbuckled from his guest room seat and kicked the chair back into the wall. It floated into place with a muted latch, restoring a smooth plane of gray. A swift tug straightened the wrinkles from his jacket as he strolled into the cargo bay. Ross lifted into an arched stretch, then dropped from the bed and followed.

"Yo, come check this out," Zoey said from the cockpit.

Max and Ross pushed through the narrow corridor and into the front cabin where Zoey and Perra leaned forward in their pilot chairs. Steve perched atop the chirping console, gazing out the panoramic viewport. Ross leapt into Perra's lap and parkoured his way up to her headrest. Max's jaw slacked open as the vista greeted his eyes.

A massive dome of blues and greens stretched across the viewport. The planet's jungle canopy reached high into the atmosphere, giving the surface an almost furry appearance. Banks of white clouds peppered the planet, several shaded gray as they dumped their bounties of rain. An enormous river system snaked across the landscape, entwining the orb under a web of cobalt blue. A pair of giant moons, also rich and lush, drifted around their colossal parent. The upper orbit teemed with ships, everything from leisure crafts to battlecruisers, all choreographed by a sophisticated traffic controller. Several stations floated in the black, reflecting sunlight off their silvery exteriors. The system churned with spacefaring activity, despite the contrast of a luscious mural beneath it.

"Wow," Max said. "It's like the Amazon on steroids."

"Before the war," Ross said with a touch of grief.

Max turned a puzzled gaze to Ross, who appeared dour for once in his life. His curiosity withered in favor of blissful ignorance.

"Now this is a pleasant surprise," Perra said, reading a hologram panel of info. "Yankar has no official language. Yarnwals are primarily explorers, so they speak whatever language is spoken. In other words, we don't have to infuse anything. They just know how to talk to everybody."

"Correct," Steve said. "We are proud communicators. Our species places a heavy emphasis on—" His undivided attention shifted to a smudge on the viewport. He ogled it with contempt and started pecking the glass, sending sharp tinks around the cabin.

Zoey rolled her eyes, nabbed him from the viewport sill, and dropped him back on her headrest. "The sooner we get you to your body, the better. Your bird-brain attention span is grating on my nerves."

"Agreed," Steve said, then flapped for balance.

The comlink crackled with an incoming feed, filling the cockpit with static before softening to the pleasant voice of a cruise ship director. "Greetings, visitors. Please prepare for a holographic transmission." Soon after, the bust of a spotted gecko bear formed above the console, donning a sharp suit and silky scarf. "Hello, friends. My name is Farina Altonyn, Yankar Ambassador. On behalf of the Yarnwal, let me be the first to welcome you to Yankar."

"Holy shit, it's a woman," Ross said, cocking his ears.

"That's sexist," Max said.

"Bite me, skin job."

"That's humanist."

Ross started to respond, but sighed and shook his head.

"There are numerous ports to choose from, both in orbit and on the surface," the recording said. A hologram map of planetary traffic replaced Farina, identifying several points of entry. "Our port authority has fed all necessary autopilot data into your navigation system.

Yankar is a non-zarking planet, so please slaughter any zarklings before arrival. All stations offer drinks, snacks, and guest services.
Should you require further assistance, feel free to consult any uniformed personnel upon landing." The map switched back to smiling
Farina. "We hope you enjoy your stay."

"My storage facility is located at the northernmost port. Gangan,
if I recall correctly."

"Got it," Perra said as she scrolled through a list of ports. She
tapped the station name, which blinked and expanded into a panel of
services. The console pinged and projected a trajectory upon the
viewport.

Steve flapped and clucked with excitement.

Zoey smiled and gripped the yoke. "Let's get you home, buddy."

The ship kicked forward with a burst of light. As they neared the
upper pole, Zoey pitched the nose and punched through the atmosphere, leaving a trail of yellow flame in their wake. The rumbles of
entry faded into a gentle hum as the vessel glided down to the surface
and sailed above the vibrant junglescape. Ribbons of white exhaust
spilled from the rear engines, connecting clouds like a needle through
fabric. The group marveled at massive trees with birch-like bark
climbing a mile above the surface. Broad leaves the size of buses
clung to every branch. Mossy vines hung from the canopy and disappeared into the thick vegetation far below. Massive rivers split the
land like watery fissures, reflecting light from a giant blue star shining
above the horizon. Flocks of winged creatures soared over open val-
leys where herds of lumbering beasts drank from river basins.

The navigation computer pinged with the approaching destination. Just ahead, a city-sized platform rested upon a monstrous pillar
that punched through the canopy. Towers of glass and metal lifted
into the clouds, as if oblivious to their lush surroundings. Ships of all
shapes and sizes circled the metropolis like bees around a hive. The
port authority pinged with autopilot acquisition. Zoey released the
yoke as the vessel slowed to a leisure taxi. The ship floated beneath
the city rim and into a tunnel of docking bays. After a series of banks
and turns, it slowed to a stop and parked itself inside a protective

cubby. A gentle push from the landing gear completed their arrival.

"Your ship has docked in bay DA-362," a robotic voice said. "Please take note for future reference."

"Got it," Perra said, tapping her comdev.

"Gravy," Zoey said as she lifted from her pilot seat.

The group filtered into the cargo bay, leaving Perra to power down the ship. Steve flapped onto a stack of crates as the rest prepped for departure. Zoey grabbed a few personal effects from a nearby locker and dropped them into a sling bag. She knocked the locker closed as Perra emerged from the cockpit. Max munched through a quick snack pack with Ross chilling by his side.

"So what's the plan, Steve-O?" Zoey said.

"We're going to Panky's Meat Parlor on the west side of the city. It's a straight shot through the tubes, not far from here."

"Sounds like a butcher's shop," Max said.

Steve shrugged. "It can be if you wait long enough."

Max cringed, then decided that any subsequent info was unwanted.

Perra skipped to the airlock, tapped it open, and swung her arm like a concierge. "Shall we?"

The group exited the ship, each dropping to the pristine platform of a swank docking bay. Yellow pathways led to a set of double doors in the rear. The walls featured rotating hologram adverts for various local businesses. The colorful print and comical characters gave them a distinct Japanese flair, gifting Max a rare glimpse of home. He grinned as the double doors slid open, revealing a crowded corridor full of alien visitors. The roar of perpetual conversation spilled into the bay. Steve waited for an opening, then hopped into the flow of traffic. The group followed one by one and the doors closed behind them.

A short way down the hall, Steve stopped at one of the many tube stations, joining a growing crowd of tourists and commuters. A train of maglev pods arrived soon after. The group pushed their way on board, squeezing together like a bundle of boglogs (the local equivalent of a can of sardines, basically a sack of screeching bog eels). Luckily for everyone, the trip was brief. They arrived at the explorer district, a shopping bazaar catering to young adventurers and crabby locals wanting to escape the humidity. The group squirmed their way through tube traffic and emerged into the city streets. Sleek shuttles cruised overhead with linear precision, passing between the towers as if attached to invisible rails. The street-level enjoyed a peaceful cleanliness with beds of vegetation and muted conversation.

Steve hopped and flapped his way across an open plaza. His excitement infected the group, elevating their pace to a light jog. They ducked and dodged their way through an assortment of scales, fur, snouts, and tails, all dressed to the nines in whatever their species deemed classy. Soon after, they arrived at the Westside branch of Panky's Meat Parlor. The backlit sign seemed out of place inside a bustling square full of blinking neon and hologram billboards, as if the shop had been there forever and the owner refused to meld with the times. Steve scratched his talons on the welcome mat, waddled inside, and flapped up to the counter. The group followed the snoodlecock into the foyer of a small shop that reminded Max of a dry cleaners. The clerk smiled through its iguana-like complexion.

"Hello friend," the clerk said, sounding like a Minnesota car salesman. "What can I do ya for?"

"Pick up, please. Should be under Gerfon Temparstangle Folinster Er Domplefoosh."

"Sure thing, one tick." The clerk whistled as he scrolled through a hologram feed. "Ah yes, there you are. Might I get a telepathic confirmation?"

Steve's eyelid twitched.

The computer pinged.

"Okay then." The clerk nodded and turned to a rack of hanging bodies. He pressed a large green button, prompting the conveyor to cycle through a collection of meat suits. The dangling humanoids, all in vegetative states, stared at the floor with blank expressions as if they had gothed-out and given up on the world. The clerk eyed each passing number and stopped at the body in question, a stumpy beast with a plump belly, resembling the unholy spawn of a chameleon and a penguin. The clerk resumed his whistle as he tapped through a sequence of commands that disconnected the life support system. He strapped on a loading belt, hoisted the body from the rack, and placed it in an open space next to the counter.

"There ya go, friend," he said, adding a shoulder pat.

Steve gave it a once over before initiating the transfer. Both bodies quivered as his consciousness jumped from the snoodlecock to the Yarnwal shell. Steve shivered inside his original meat sack, then blinked and smacked his lips as if waking from a long nap. After a grunt and shoulder roll, he patted his belly in familiar comfort. "Hello, old friend," he said in his baritone documentary voice.

The snoodlecock, having no fucking clue where it was, spun around the countertop in total confusion. It flinched at every new face, then yelped and jerked backwards when it eyed the green clerk, paralyzing it with a potent mixture of fear and bewilderment.

Steve smiled and scooped the bird from the counter with a gentle hand. "Thank you for the glorious adventure," he said, then gobbled the snoodlecock whole. The bird shrieked as it fell into his gullet. Steve gulped, belched, and sighed with contentment. He wiped his mouth and rubbed his belly before catching the horrified faces of everyone else (minus the clerk, who expected such things).

"Dude!" Max said. "You just ate ... yourself!"

"Bird ain't me no more," Steve said with a flat tone.

"Yeah, but ..." Perra struggled to conjure a reasonable retort. "That was, kind of, weird."

"I'm a fleshless cyborg devoid of nutritional properties," Ross said in a hurried voice. "Just wanted to throw that out there."

"Aaaanyway," Zoey said, extending her hand. "It's nice to finally meet the real you, Steve."

"The pleasure is all mine," he said, gripping her hand. "Words cannot express my profound gratitude for all you have done for me."

"We owed you," Perra said. "And thank you again for saving our butts. Twice."

Steve grinned, then belched up a few feathers.

"Seriously," Max said to Ross. "That's messed up."

Ross maintained his horrified *please don't eat me* stare.

"And to show my appreciation for bringing me all this way, I would like to extend an invitation to my home this evening. It is a time-honored tradition on Yankar for families to celebrate the glorious returns of their explorers. We shall dance, drink, and drink some more. I shall feed and house you all as my guests of honor." Steve stretched his face into a toothy grin.

The group traded smirking glances, minus a wide-eyed Ross who feared a sudden snack attack.

"We would be delighted," Perra said with a warm smile.

"Excellent!" Steve chuckled and clapped his paws, which bounced a pudgy belly.

The clerk cleared his throat. "This is touching and all, but you do know you're still naked, right?" He opened a storage bin and set a stack of clothes on the counter.

An awkward silence gripped the parlor.

Steve glanced at the clothes, then down to his birthday suit, then back to the group. His lips puckered as he battled a sudden loss of dignity. "Yes, um ... excuse me." He swiped the pile from the counter and hurried to a nearby changing room.

* * *

That evening, the group arrived at Steve's home, a tiny cottage town tucked deep inside the forest. The community relished all the modern conveniences, but suffered none of the hassles. Many tribes preferred simpler living as a direct opposition to the hustle and bustle of platform cities. The sights and sounds of the jungle captivated those who sought a more intimate connection with the planet. They enjoyed an endless bounty of fresh food and clean water, collected from a vibrant landscape with minimal effort. Steve's community dated back untold generations, all in love with the forest.

Steve's family greeted his arrival like a victorious king returning from battle. His relatives, many of whom occupied new bodies, welcomed the Earthling, feline, and Mulgawats like wearied travelers in need of pampering. They feasted on beast and vine, exploring an endless variety of strange yet delicious flavors. They also drank, a lot, draining barrels of wine and ale. Max had very little experience with alcohol, even less so with exotic brews from other planets. Thus, he drank himself to the point of complete stupefaction. It was the greatest party of his life, and he savored every second.

Later that evening, after most of the family had called it a night, Zoey, Perra, Max, and Steve sat around a dwindling bonfire. Ross had wandered off in search of a safe place to sleep, for fear of midnight snackers. The group barked and laughed about their recent adventure, toasting the highs and scoffing the lows. Max teetered upon a log while wearing a cheeky grin. He raised his mug and shouted "I love lizard Hobbiton!" before falling backwards and passing out.

CHAPTER 17

Max awoke the next morning with a raging hangover. The pops of crackling embers from a burnt-out bonfire needled his ears, exacerbating a throbbing headache. He lay where he fell the night before, sprawled out in the grass with a log tucked beneath his legs. Twitching eyelids lifted like faulty window blinds, revealing a bright blue sky overhead with banks of fluffy white clouds. A lush green canopy of giant leaves and soaring trees swayed on the peripherals of an open valley. The chirps of birds and barks of other strange creatures echoed in the distance. He groaned, smacked his lips, and lifted himself back onto the log.

As he struggled with a rousing soberness, he stared into the fire pit like a wizard seeking guidance. Orange fissures glowed through a pane of gray ash. A few logs remained as little more than charred twigs of coal. Max yawned, rubbed his eyes, and scratched an itch under his bushy beard. His jaw slacked open as he glanced down to a scruffy chin mane resting atop a rugged shirt. Long, unkempt hair dangled in front of his face, hooking his attention. He slid dirty fingers through the nappy locks and gave them a tug. A sharp sting confirmed that the strands were indeed his.

He continued to examine his peculiar new ensemble. A complete set of grimy leather duds clung to his body, like a ratty biker after a mud wrestling match. Thick straps and heavy stitching gave them an air of durability, the kind of clothes that outlasted the bodies they cover. Sandy brown pants fell to a pair of fur-lined boots that hugged his legs just above the ankle. No heels or cowboy flair, just a thick hide with latching straps to keep them taut. A beaded necklace with large claws completed the outfit. Max lifted the strand for a closer look. Sharp talons shined with colorful patterns, as if clipped from a fashion-forward Velociraptor.

Max dropped his palms onto the log and started to lift his body, but paused at an unusual sight. The arm press had flexed an epic pair of biceps, something wholly foreign to his gamer physique. He stiffened his posture and struck a few bodybuilder poses, or rather, what a lanky nerd considered bodybuilder poses. Another flex lifted a slab of meat under his shirt. He hooked his collar and pulled it open, revealing an impressive pair of pecs. An eager hand slipped under the shirt and fondled one of them with the same enthusiasm of reaching second base. A slap of his thigh uncovered a sturdy trunk of lean muscle. Max chuckled at the discovery, like a would-be superhero waking up after a radioactive spider bite.

Max climbed to his feet with the aid of his new beefcake body. He surveyed the valley for any rational explanation, but the entire community had vanished. No huts, no roads, no walkways, no vehicles of any kind. It was the same spot, as far as he could tell, but engulfed by trees and foliage. The tiny clearing he occupied seemed exposed, dangerous even. A thin line of smoke lifted from the fire pit, over which hung a roasting spit and a charred rib cage. Even the dull roar of space ships cruising through the atmosphere had vanished. He glanced up to the open sky, looking for signs of modern life, but found nothing. Moments later, a winged creature the size of a prop plane sailed across the valley. A mixture of scales and feathers gave it a mangled look, like the mutated offspring of a cockatoo and pterodactyl. The beast shrieked as it passed, sending a bitter chill down Max's spine.

Panic set in hard and fast. Max grabbed a sturdy-looking spear resting beside the pit and sprinted towards the shuttle station a few miles away. The sun disappeared overhead as he exited the valley and entered a dense jungle. The lack of roads forced him to carve his own path using nothing but wits and a fuzzy memory. He ducked under branches, leapt over roots, and splashed across babbling brooks. Leaves and bugs smacked him in the face, but a focused stride kept his attention forward. Despite having never worked out a day in his life, Max raced through the brush without breaking a sweat. The newfound endurance took him by surprise. A welcome tweak for sure, but it failed to explain what the hell was going on.

Max hugged a bend at full speed and skidded to a halt where the shuttle station should have been. An anxious gaze darted around the area, but found a barren hill of rocks and dirt. A distinctive boulder confirmed that he was in the right place. He huffed with frustration and scratched his noggin, unable to make sense of the situation.

"Hello?!" he said, sending an echo through the trees.

Silence responded.

"Is there anybody out there?!"

Twig snaps responded.

Max whipped his gaze up the hill to find a pair of eyes staring back at him. A tarantula beast the size of a monster truck crested the summit. Bulging yellow orbs and rows of jagged teeth adorned the face of a hairy nightmare. It roared in a manner that buckled Max's knees and came charging down the hill. Max yelped, spun around, and sprinted back the way he had come. The thumps of skittering limbs shook the ground behind him. Max's leg muscles burned with a rush of adrenaline, pushing him as fast as humanly possible, but not fast enough. The creature gained on its prey, closer, and closer, then a chomp and blood-curdling screech.

Max tumbled to the ground and spun to face the beast with his spear at the ready, only to find it lifting into the air in the massive jaws of a furry dinosaur. The towering creature, resembling Godzilla with a yeti complex, stood as tall as an office building. Its massive legs mimicked the trees it stood among in size and color, a very effective hunting strategy. Max understood right away that the monster just hung out and waited patiently for treats to wander by. The tarantula flailed and growled before a mammoth chomp crushed its brittle body. Yellow blood rained from the sky as the dino crunched through the exoskeleton. Max quivered as warm droplets kissed his cheeks and chest. While grateful for the deus ex machina life extension, he took the opportunity to slip away unnoticed.

Max glided over a hill and ducked behind a tree to catch his breath. He gripped the spear with both hands, cradling it to his chest like a toddler with a favorite toy. Gasping and panting, he stood with his back to the massive trunk as his lungs talked each other off the ledge. He closed his eyes and concentrated on slowing his heart to a reasonable rhythm. The horror began to fade, but then a tickle on his shoulder popped his eyes open. Lips clenched as he slogged his gaze to the side. A giant blue centipede the size of a pool noodle crawled down his arm. It paused to return the stare, using lanky red eyestalks. Max yelped, flail-punched the creature off his arm, and leapt back into a full sprint.

A short time later, Max arrived back at the valley edge. He poked his spear through a drapery of vines and pulled them aside like a shower curtain. The sunlight warmed his skin as he stepped into the valley, his heart still racing from the hideous misadventure. His lungs slowed to a moderate pace, restoring an air of composure. He lifted a hand to his brow and scanned the grassy plane from end to end. Near the center, a ribbon of smoke continued to lift from the fire pit. The sounds of a vibrant forest filled the air, everything from croaking trees to yapping creatures. Max sighed and crept along the forest line, heeding a powerful need to stay hidden.

Soon after, he happened upon a puddle of water. Max dropped to his knees and scooped handfuls into his mouth, quenching a sudden thirst. Looming over the puddle edge, he watched the ripples smooth to reveal a jarring reflection. A curious hand caressed soiled cheeks and traced a meaty jaw. He opened his mouth wide, uncovering stained teeth in desperate need of a dental hygienist.

"Jeez. I look like a Viking hobo."

Climbing to his feet, he continued his slow hike around the valley until he found a fallen log to rest upon. A wearied body took a much-needed seat as lungs expelled a cache of pent-up air. He studied the spear he carried, a crude device with dried blood stains on a stony head. An armpit sniff and subsequent recoil verified that he hadn't bathed in weeks, maybe months. He set the spear aside, lifted his gaze to the sky, and sighed with vexation.

"Where the hell am I?"

A rustle in the bushes needled his ear. He whipped his gaze to the brush behind him, flinging beads of sweat into the dirt. Grabbing his spear, he leapt from the log and spun to face an unknown menace. Another rustle, closer this time. He hardened his gate with spear primed and ready. Lungs fluttered. Muscles trembled. Another rustle, this time with a low grumble. Max whimpered. Leaves exploded into the air as a saber-toothed tiger burst through the foliage and landed with a thud. The creature locked eyes with the human and roared with fury, exposing powerful fangs. Max shrieked, dropped his spear, and sprinted into the open field. The cat hesitated, toying with its prey before digging its claws into the earth and giving chase.

Max reached full sprint in a matter of seconds, but with nowhere to hide and death closing in, he pushed towards the fire pit in hopes of wielding the roasting spit. The cat's thumping stride grew louder and louder with each passing second. Max glanced over his shoulder, only to stare down the bulging eyes and galloping legs of his impending doom. He whipped his gaze back to the pit, now a stone's throw away, but caught the edge of a boulder underfoot. His legs crossed and buckled, sending him tumbling to the ground and skidding to a halt. A cloud of dust infected the air as he flipped to his back and raised bloodied palms over his face. The beast planted its paws to either side and loomed over the human with sadistic intent. Hot, musky breath flowed between a pair of massive fangs. Slitted green eyes pierced its prey through a thick mane of bronze fur. Max cowered beneath the creature, helpless and shaking. The cat roared, stretched its mouth wide, and came down upon its victim.

Max screamed.

But nothing happened.

He opened his eyes and peeked over trembling arms to find the beast standing over him, only with playful eyes and a puckered grin.

"Gotcha," it said with a British accent.

The feline burst into laughter and leapt off to the side, leaving Max in a state of paralyzed confusion. It rolled on the ground and cackled like a jackass while Max struggled to make sense of the situation.

"You should have seen your face," the beast said while slowing to a chuckle. "Classic."

Max narrowed his eyes, lifted to a seated position, and slogged his gaze over to the feline. "Ra—Ross?"

"No, your mum."

Max glanced into the field, then back to Ross, then back into the field, then up to the sky, then back to Ross. "What the fucking fuck?"

"Good question."

"Why are you a tiger?"

"Also a good question."

"And where the hell are we?"

"An even better question."

Max responded with puzzled silence.

"We're still on Yankar."

Max added a twitching eyelid.

Ross grumbled and shook his head. "You shifted while occupying a complex domain, you silly prat. I thought you would have figured this out by now. Never shift on a planet that you don't want to inhabit for the rest of your life. You've been a lucky knob thus far, but not this time. Now you're stuck on a primitive version of Yankar, one where the Yarnwal never evolved. And how many versions of this rock do you think they exist on? Bloody few, that's how many. I swear, one of these days I'm going to smack you across the cheek with a dead—"

"Wait, wait, just, wait a goddamn minute." Max took a deep breath, gathered his wits, and steadied his voice. "How the hell are *you* still here?"

Ross cocked an ear back. "Oh, right, *that*." He cleared his throat and glanced away, as if ashamed. "Well, my friend, I guess there's something you should know about me."

THE END

The story continues with:
Max and the Banjo Ferret

Zachry Wheeler is an award-winning science fiction novelist, screenwriter, and coffee slayer. He enjoys English football, stand-up comedy, and is known to lurk around museums and brewpubs. His series works include the *Immortal Wake* and *Max and the Multiverse*.

Learn more at **ZachryWheeler.com**

If you enjoyed this nutty tale, please consider posting a short review on Amazon. Ratings and reviews are the currency by which authors gain visibility. They are the single greatest way to show your support and keep us writing the stories that you love.

Thank you for reading!

CPSIA information can be obtained
at www.ICGtesting.com
Printed in the USA
BVHW031918271120
594367BV00026B/157